ONE HUNDRED GLANCES

AN ASPEN COVE SMALL TOWN ROMANCE

KELLY COLLINS

BOOK NOOK PRESS

CHAPTER ONE

For the last six months, Sosie Grant had tossed out prayers like spare pennies at the Trevi Fountain, but not one was answered.

"There's got to be something in the studio you can sell," Sosie said, as Theresa drove toward Aspen Cove.

"I'm your agent, not a sorceress. Knowing you, you started dozens of projects but finished none."

Sosie shifted in her seat until her head laid on the soft leather facing the driver's side. On a deep inhale, she took in the lemon and leather scent.

"Is this a new car?" She touched the soft leather of the seat with her fingertips. Theresa must have been doing okay to have a new SUV.

"Nope, it's the same one as before, but I just had it detailed. Sometimes a little cleaning up of one's life is a good thing; it puts you on a better path."

Sosie knew her comment was purposeful. A reminder that the road she was traveling led to a dead end. "I'm not a car."

"No, but you need a way to keep moving on."

Sosie ignored the comment. To move forward meant leaving the past behind, and she wasn't ready to do that. "Do you remember when I was a kid, and I could draw on a napkin, and everyone clamored to buy them?"

"I do, but you're not a cute two-year-old prodigious artist anymore. You're a thirty-year-old with a lot to figure out. The first being how to come up with ten to twelve pieces to put in the gallery. If you can't deliver that, we are both in breach of contract. I'm not going down because you planned poorly."

"I didn't plan this. You can be such a bitch sometimes. It's a wonder you have any clients with that attitude. Don't forget, you work for me." She was so tired of Theresa harping at her. It wasn't as if she controlled her life or situation. Some things were simply out of her hands.

"I've never looked at it that way. I've always thought of it as you working for me. I'm the broker between you and the client. Without me, you wouldn't have anything."

The car swerved, and Sosie's head hit the glass.

"Your thought process has always been a bit skewed."

"Don't forget, you also have to pay back the advance to the Albright family. What did you do with the money, anyway?"

"Do you even have to ask?" She rubbed at the sore spot on the back of her head where it collided with the window.

"Rehab again?" The sound of Theresa hitting the steering wheel with her palm filled the air. "How many times are you going to put your brother in a facility before you realize Gage won't stop drinking?"

"As long as it takes for him to stop drinking." Theresa would never understand her situation or the pain her brother had to go through because he was born her brother. How does a kid who is wonderful and beautiful but average by most standards live in a home where a two-year-old paints like Monet the first time she picks up a brush?

How is he supposed to shine when the world only cares about her, Sosie, the girl who everyone thinks is the reincarnation of one of the greats?

2

"Stop blaming yourself for the failures of your parents. They had two children. Hell, I have three, and all of them are different. I've got a nurse, an architect, and a fast-food cashier. I don't love one more than the other. I may love them individually, but that's because none of them are the same. Each one brings something unique to the world and to my life."

"My mother wasn't a failure. You have no idea what you're talking about."

"Your parents should be the ones driving you to Aspen Cove to pick up your stuff, not me."

Sosie shrugged. "Mom's in Europe, and I haven't seen Dad in years." She touched her finger to her chin, thinking about the last time she'd heard from her father. "I got a card from Dad for my birthday. The postmark was from Jamaica."

"That's my point. They should be here. After your accident, they were nowhere to be found."

Sosie wanted to roll her eyes, but somehow it seemed ridiculous. "Lyme disease is not an accident."

"It's an undesirable and unfortunate happening, and by that definition, it's an accident."

A loud grumble filled the SUV, and Sosie gripped her stomach.

"Didn't you eat?" Theresa asked.

A low growl vibrated from her throat. "I'm lucky I got dressed. By the way, you didn't even comment on my outfit." She pulled her phone from her bag. "Did you know they have an app that helps with that?"

"They have one for everything these days. Even my watch tells me when to breathe as if my body won't know that on its own." Theresa sighed. "At least you match."

"I figured as long as I wear black or blue on the bottom, everything else works on top."

"For a woman whose life is all about color, you're the worst at picking out clothes. Ever hear of the color wheel?"

"I address color differently. For me, it comes from a more intuitive perspective." Her stomach rumbled again. "If I don't get something to eat right away, I'll turn a horrid shade of green and be sick. Then your SUV won't smell like lemons and leather."

"I thought we'd eat at that diner you're always talking about."

"Maisey's Diner is great, but I won't make it that far. I need something to tide me over."

"Girl, you are such a mess."

Sosie hung her head. "I know."

Not too far down, Theresa pulled off the road, and they coasted to a stop.

"A gas station is the best I can do. What do you want?"

Sosie reached down and felt around for her purse. "Anything with sugar will work." She rummaged inside her bag for her wallet, but Theresa lost her patience and exited the car before Sosie could offer her money.

She realized she was walking a tightrope with her agent. They were friendly, but never friends. She had invested little time cultivating long-term relationships because she spent most of her life in front of a canvas. Even growing up, she didn't get out much unless her mother forced a trip on her. Yes, April Grant tried to bring balance into a life where there was none, but Sosie was a recluse and stayed in most days. School events and socials didn't interest her. Weekends weren't filled with movie theater popcorn or county fair cotton candy; instead, the scent of paints and linseed oil covered her like a comforting cloak since she could walk.

The driver's side door opened, and Theresa thrust a banana into her hand.

"Natural sugar is better for you."

"Now you're my mom?"

"If I was your mom, you wouldn't be in the pickle you're in."

Every once in a while, Theresa's sixty-odd years showed in her vernacular. "No one says pickle these days." Sosie peeled the banana and took a bite. "Maybe jam. I wouldn't be in the jam I'm in if you were my mother."

Theresa gunned the engine, kicking up gravel in her wake. "If I were your mother, I would have put money aside for you instead of gallivanting across the world."

Sosie took the last bite of banana and rolled the peel into a cylinder. Before she could shove it in the cup holder, Theresa took it from her hand and rolled down her window.

"You didn't just toss that outside, did you?"

"It's biodegradable. Now back to your mom."

"My mother took me places to broaden my horizons—to show me perspective. It helped my art." It also helped her mind. Her mother understood the pressures of the art world and made sure she had well-timed respites. Sadly, during a trip, her father found another woman and created a new family. Somewhere deep inside, Sosie took the blame for that. It was why she was hell-bent on making sure her mother had a good life now.

"Oh, stop defending her. She took you places so she could travel on your dime. You paid for every one of those trips with the sale of each painting." Theresa's voice grew more forceful with every word. "Do you think she bought a villa in Tuscany for your benefit? No, she used your earnings to finance it, but who's living there free and clear while you're struggling to make ends meet?"

Sosie scrubbed at her face. "That villa saved my mother's life. She had nothing when my father left her—nothing."

"At least she has a life. If you had nourished your soul as much as your art, you might not be alone. There might be a husband here to help you."

"A husband ... really?" She turned to face Theresa. It was funny that she'd suggest Sosie take time for love when she kept pushing her for art. It didn't matter much because she saw firsthand what love could do. "The last thing I need is a husband to remind me I have no value but my skill as an artist. Besides, I have you for that. Love isn't for me."

"Don't mix me in with the lot. It's your mother, brother, and father who reminds you that your only value is your art and what money you earn from it to help them. Love is out there Sosie, you just need to be open to it."

"Come on, that's not true, especially now. Besides, who would want to tackle this." She said waving her hand up and down in front of herself. "As for my parents, they haven't taken a cent from me since I turned eighteen. It's been a dozen years. Let it go."

"When you turned eighteen, they walked away. Why is that?"

"I was an adult." The sun shining through the window warmed her skin, filling her with memories of her childhood home in Estes Park, and the days she spent painting in the sunroom next to her mother, who never asked her for anything. Yes, her art kept a roof over their heads and food in their bellies, but that was because their father failed to provide for his family. He was the one with his palm out, making sure that his contribution to the DNA pool was compensated for.

"No, it's because you were no longer the cute prodigy. You blended into the woodwork and didn't stand out. A toddler artist is a rare find, but now, you're simply not as special. You were a lame horse that they couldn't ride any longer."

Tears streamed down Sosie's cheeks. She hated to cry because it was a waste of time. Not once in the last six months had it helped when she wept, so why bother now? "Why are you so mean?"

"I'm not being mean, I'm being honest. It's something you'll need to be as well. Your life is not the same, and it won't ever be the same, so you better prepare for it."

She didn't want Theresa to see how much her words hurt, so she shifted to face the window. Nothing but silence filled the car for the rest of the trip. Closing her eyes, she prayed for this day to be over because cleaning out her studio was like saying goodbye to an old friend.

She wished she could have tackled the situation on her own, but she needed help. There wasn't much she could do autonomously. Who knew how much a tiny tick bite could change a life?

"We're here." Theresa drove the SUV into a parking spot, killed the engine, and climbed out.

Sosie grabbed her purse and opened the door. Immediately, the scent of bacon and maple syrup wafted past her. It was the smell of happiness and brought back memories of a time when things were easier, and life was worth living.

She swung her legs out the door and rose to her feet. On the first step forward, she rolled her ankle, where the sidewalk had sunk from the curb. She fell hard on her hip and sat in stunned silence.

"Let me help you." Theresa lifted Sosie's purse to her shoulder and pulled her up. She closed the SUV door and led her into the diner.

"Are you okay?" Theresa brushed away whatever was on the leg of her pants and helped her into the booth before taking the seat across from her. "Did you hurt anything?"

"My pride."

"Well, you've got plenty more of that stored up, even if you have little else."

The smell of Maisey's signature perfume hit her before the woman arrived. It was a strong honeysuckle scent that mixed nicely with the sweetness of the maple syrup surrounding her.

"Well, if it isn't Miss Sosie Grant."

Sosie turned her head up. "Hey, Maisey." She never drew attention to the changes in her since the "accident" as

Theresa called it. She found if she acted normal, people rarely noticed.

"Where have you been?" Maisey asked.

Where did she begin? The story was far too long to recite. "I've been busy in Denver."

"Too busy to come up and say hello?"

She hung her head. "I apologize. My life has been a whirlwind the last few months."

Theresa slapped her hand on the table, rattling the silverware. "She's—"

"Starving." Sosie broke in. "I'd die for a cola and one of Ben's famous burgers."

"Make that two," said Theresa.

"Coming right up." Maisey's shoes squeaked on the floor as she walked away.

"Why are you lying to her?"

"I'm not lying to anyone." She bristled with indignation.

"Not true, you're lying to yourself. People need to know what happened."

She shook her head. "No one needs to know my business. It's my business." She hoped her raised voice didn't draw attention, so she leaned into the center of the table. "Just let me have this moment where my life seems normal. I'm only asking for a minute. Can't you give me that?"

"Your life will never be normal again."

"So, you keep reminding me."

"Here you go." Maisey set the cola on the table with a clunk. "Your burgers will be ready in a few. I'll be back in a minute to chat. I want to know what you've been up to."

"Will you tell her you've spent a great deal of time in the hospital and at a facility in San Francisco? What about the fact that you no longer paint, but sit in a dark room sipping tea and crying?"

"Will you shut the hell up? This is my life, and I'll handle it."

"That's the problem. You're not handling it. You're waiting for a miracle, and the world is fresh out of them. There are no answers for you."

"I'm not giving up."

"You gave up the day you got your diagnosis."

Everything burned, including her eyes. Her skin heated from the anger boiling inside her veins. Life was so damn unfair, and she didn't need Theresa making it worse. "Why are you here?"

"Because you've got no one else, and you need me."

The truth of that statement hollowed her out, but she refused to play the victim. "No, you need me. You need the last of my work so you can sell it and get your commission. You don't care about me, which makes you no different from my father. My value to you is nothing beyond the money you earn from my work. You're here because if I don't deliver the Albright project, or the paintings for the gallery exhibit, your reputation will suffer."

"I won't lie to you and tell you that's not true, but only partially so. I'm here because if someone doesn't help you out, you have no hope for a life."

Feeling like the girl from *Firestarter*, Sosie closed her eyes and willed her temper back. *Back off. Back off.* She reached for her soda in hopes of a cool down but misjudged the distance and sent the glass toppling over. Cola splashed everywhere, running off the edge of the Formica top and onto her lap. She jolted up from the icy cold hit and scrambled from the booth, running into the table beside her. Her hand came down for balance, but she hit a plate, sending its contents into the air. Splats of food dotted her face.

"Holy hell," a man's voice shouted. "Watch what you're doing."

"I can't, asshole. I'm blind."

CHAPTER TWO

Baxter stared up at the woman with hauntingly beautiful blue eyes. Eyes that seemed to look into his soul and yet couldn't see a thing.

"I'm so sorry. I didn't know." A blob of mashed potatoes unstuck itself from his T-shirt and rolled down to sit in his lap. He ignored the mess and examined her. "Are you okay? I mean, outside of losing your balance, did you hurt yourself?"

"I'm fine. I just ... I haven't quite gotten used to my situation, and I lose my bearings."

He looked past her to the older woman sitting in the booth and lifted his brow as if to ask, "Is she really okay?"

With a flourish of her hand, the woman said, "Oh, she's fine. It probably bruised her ego, but she's got a massive one, so no worries."

He rose from his chair and watched the clump of mashed potatoes hit the floor with a splat.

"Was that your lunch?" Sosie asked.

He chuckled. "Yep, but I'm sure my aunt will replace it." He stuck his hand out to shake hers but dropped it and shook his head. "I'm Baxter Black."

She cocked her head to the side and opened her eyes wide. For a woman who couldn't see, she had an expressive gaze.

"Any relation to Riley?"

"She's my sister." He noticed the gravy on the back of her hand and reached for his napkin. "It seems as if my food found its way to you. Let me help clean you up."

She raised her hand as if to look at it. "I'm pretty sure it's the other way around, and my hand found your food."

He wasn't sure what the right protocol was. Did he wipe off what he saw or hand her the napkin and let her do it herself? Sadly, he failed miserably with caretaking and didn't have a clue.

When the tip of the napkin hit her skin, she closed her palm around it and she took over, wiping her hand clean.

Turning from left to right, she inhaled and huffed. "Can you please turn me in the direction I came from?"

Maisey rushed over with two plates of burgers and fries. "Haven't I told you before that there are no food fights allowed in the diner?" She tried to sound firm, but the giggle in her voice gave her away. "Let me wipe the table." She left to get a wet terry cloth, and once the booth was wiped clean and dried, Maisey helped the woman back to her seat. "Why didn't you say anything, Sosie? I wondered what could keep you from your art. Now I know."

He watched Sosie wince from the statement.

"Can I borrow that towel?" he asked Maisey. When she handed it to him, he cleaned the surrounding mess but kept an ear tuned to the conversation happening beside him.

"It's not something I'm happy about, but I'm coming to terms with what this has done to me and my life."

"Don't let her fool you," said the lady who was still sitting in the booth. "She hasn't reconciled with her disability. That's the problem. She's in denial."

"Geez, Theresa, give me a break. Don't pretend like you

care." Sosie plopped onto the red pleather bench. She blindly felt the table until her fingers reached the fries. "All you care about is the paycheck."

"I'll be back," Maisey turned and looked at him. "I'll get you another plate, Baxter. Hang tight."

He pushed his near-empty plate to the side and listened for what would happen with Theresa and Sosie. It was like a late-night drama unfolding in front of him.

"I'm so tired of your shit, Sosie. You're blind, not dead. The problem with you is you're spoiled. Someone has doted on you all of your life. They've treated you like a golden child. What you need is some tough love."

"Love? You think you're qualified to give it to me?"

The older woman tossed her napkin on the table. "You bet your ass I am. You'll never get past this if people keep fixing things for you. You came to clean out your studio. Do it yourself." Theresa rose from the table and stomped away.

Several words passed through his brain. There was the name Sosie, which sounded familiar but add in the word art and studio, and he knew exactly who she was. Sosie Grant, the artist, was back in Aspen Cove, and she was blind.

He watched as a tear slipped down her cheek. Just as he was about to get up and move into the booth across from her, Wes showed up.

"Sorry I'm late."

Taking his eyes from Sosie was like trying to separate two fingers stuck together with superglue. It was hard and painful, but not impossible.

"Hey, Wes." He pointed to the seat across from him and hoped it was clean. "Sorry for the mess, I had a little mishap."

Out of the corner of his eye, he saw Sosie turn his way. Her mouth opened and closed several times before it snapped shut. Maybe she thought better of confessing. She moved the fries around her plate until she picked one up and took a bite. She stared straight ahead as if her life hadn't just gone up in flames.

He turned back to Wes, who had a smirk on his face. "Do you want to be alone?" He shifted his eyes to Sosie.

"Nope. Let's get down to business."

Wes put a folder on the table and opened it. Inside were several contracts. "With the band in town, and the sheriff hiring a new deputy, we've got plenty to keep us busy over the next few months. I've got the Lockharts working on the bigger projects. The Cooper brothers did the teardowns and rebuilds, but I thought you'd like the detail work. Since you did such an amazing job on B's Book Nook, I saved the finishing touches for you."

He considered the pile of contracts in front of Wes. It was what he needed and what he dreaded. The work would give him a paycheck, but it would also keep him busy—maybe too busy to complete his home. It was an endless cycle of want and need. He wanted to finish his house, but he needed the money and time to do it. He couldn't complete one without the other.

Wes took the papers and spread them out on the table. "Most of the guys in the band are used to modern amenities like steam showers and jacuzzi tubs, and that requires demolition and restoration. Owen has his brothers Paxton and Eli finishing those bigger projects. Sheriff Cooper hired a new deputy named Merrick, who bought the house on Rose Lane. It's got good bones, but it needs some serious TLC." He pointed to the number at the top of the form. "Call him, and he'll tell you what he wants done."

"Am I working for him, or for you?" It made a difference only as far as payment went. Wes paid him by the hour, whereas he got paid by the job otherwise.

"You're working for me. I built the cost of your labor into the house. I figured that would be better for both of us."

"Okay, how do you want me to attack this list? Is there an order of priority?"

"I'd start with the band, the Coopers Green House builds. They're doing a Fourth of July concert in Hope Park, besides the annual Fireman's Fundraiser at the end of the summer. I think it's important to make them happy since they bring a lot to the town as far as tourism dollars. Start with the Coopers Green House builds. There's a lot of intricate work like moldings, tile, fixtures, and then move on to Merrick's place or split your time between the two. It doesn't really matter as long as it all gets done. Merrick's house needs to be gutted, but he likes the feel of the old home and wants to stay true to the era."

"Basically, it's a money pit." Baxter knew what that was like. His bungalow was the same, but there was something nostalgic about respecting the workmanship of a home built nearly a hundred years ago. "I'll get on this right away."

Maisey walked by and put a new blue-plate special on the table in front of him.

"Can I get you anything, Wes?"

"No, ma'am. I'm was just heading out."

"You tell that wife of yours I'm making her favorite chocolate silk pie this afternoon."

Wes nodded. "I will. Lydia loves your pie."

Instead of making the rounds of the restaurant like she normally did, Maisey took a seat across from Sosie. An uneaten burger and fries left by Theresa sat in front of her.

"Now, tell me what's going on."

Baxter dug into his mashed potatoes and gravy but kept an ear tuned in to the conversation beside him. The turn of events was fascinating. Not much happened in Aspen Cove that was newsworthy, but a blind painter showing up in town was interesting considering the last time she was here, she could see.

He knew the name because his sister had mentioned her studio. When Riley's workspace went up in flames, she worried that Sosie's art would be destroyed by smoke or water. Neither happened because Samantha put the necessary safety precautions into The Guild Creative Center that protected everyone. Each studio was independent and had its own safety system. A fire in one didn't mean water in all.

"I don't know where to begin," Sosie said. Her voice was soft—almost a whisper. "It started with Lyme disease and went on from there." She moved her hands in the air as she spoke. "They said it wasn't permanent, or they didn't think it was. Optic neuritis is what they call the condition. It's basically swelling of the optic nerve, but it's been six months, and there's been no change."

Maisey slid her hand over Sosie's in a motherly way. Or, at least that's what Baxter thought a mother would do. His mom had abandoned him and Riley at birth, so he wasn't sure how a mother would nurture a child. His stepmother was kind enough to him, but she often abused Riley with ugly words and disregard. Outside of movies, they had no scale on which to gauge motherly devotion.

He shook the thought from his mind and focused on the conversation happening between Sosie and Maisey.

"What are you going to do?"

Sosie shrugged. "What can I do? I came here with my agent to clean out the studio."

Maisey looked around. "Where did she go?"

"I don't know, but she'll be back. I can't imagine she'd actually leave me in the diner. She has a financial interest in what's left in my studio."

"I'm sure you're right." Maisey patted her hand and rose. "I need to get to work." She looked toward the kitchen. "Orders are backing up, and Ben won't be happy with me." She slid from the booth. "You eat while I'll get you another soda." Maisey picked up the empty glass and left.

Baxter finished his meal and left fifteen dollars on the table to cover his bill and a tip. Before he walked out, he stopped by Sosie's table.

"Umm, it was nice meeting you."

She turned her head and lifted her chin, so she was facing him. Her eyes were full of emotion; he saw despair and hurt and loss deep within those magnetic blue irises.

"Nice meeting you, too. I promise if we meet again not to toss your food around like an angry ape." She lifted her hand to her nose. "Mashed potatoes and gravy?"

He chuckled. "Yep, how did you know."

She sat for a long second and licked her lips. "I'd like to say it was my other senses kicking in, but I'm afraid I haven't learned to compensate yet." She smiled, and the entire room lit up. "I got a taste when I overturned your plate and your food took flight. I might order that next time."

He wasn't sure what to do. How did he convey his feelings without using expressive body language? If it were anyone else, he probably would have rolled his eyes, but if he did that, she'd miss the gesture.

"Tell you what, next time you want a bite, just ask."

"I will. Nice meeting you, Baxter. Tell your sister, I said hello."

He glanced out the front window. "Are you sure your agent is coming back?"

She sighed. "She'll be back. I've never known her to pass up a payday."

"Okay then. Good luck to you."

Her lips quivered as she pulled them into a smile. "That's all I have left."

As he walked away, he wondered what his life would be like if he ever lost the use of his eyes, and the only word that came to mind was over.

CHAPTER THREE

She isn't coming back.

Sosie sat in the booth for hours nursing her soda and her bruised heart. She dug into her second piece of pie, but eating so much sugar only gave her a bellyache.

"Can I get you anything else, sweetheart?" Maisey asked.

A dozen things went through her mind, but none of them would solve her current problem.

"No, thank you. Umm, I should probably vacate this booth so someone else can have it."

A hand touched her shoulder. "Oh, honey, you can stay all day and night in this booth, and I wouldn't care."

Sosie laughed to avoid tears. "I may have to. I'm in a bit of pickle here." She found it funny to have used the saying she'd given Theresa such a hard time about, but it sounded right. She was in a tight spot and didn't know how to get herself out. "Do you have the number for the bed-and-breakfast?"

Maisey made a tsk tsk sound that Sosie knew was accompanied by some kind of facial expression that said are-you-kidding-me. Of course, Maisey would have the number memorized because Ben's son Cannon was with the owner.

"I know it by heart, but if you're looking for a room, it won't do you any good. They're booked up past September."

"Right, that makes sense. It's the tourist season."

"Oh, honey, ever since Samantha came into town, it's tourist season all year. People drive up just to get a glimpse of my daughter-in-law, and now with the band moving here, it's pure chaos."

"They got married?" Sosie was so out of touch with everyone and everything around her.

"They sure did. They did it Vegas-style with rhinestones and Elvis. There's lots that's happened since you've been gone." The air shifted. "Sage and Cannon got married and got pregnant." Maisey's voice came from across the booth. "Sage is due around Thanksgiving."

"That's amazing. You'll be a grandma again."

"I will. We also have a new bookstore where the old Dry Goods Store used to be. It's called B's Book Nook, and the owner is Jake Powers, who's a famous life coach." She leaned in and whispered. "He's got Brandy's kidney."

While she didn't know much about the town or its people, it was hard to avoid hearing stories about Bea Bennett and the death of her daughter, Brandy.

"Wow, that's crazy."

"Right? But he's such a good man, and by all accounts, a wizard at helping people sort out their lives."

His name wasn't familiar. "I might need his help."

"You just might. He's with Natalie and her brother, Will." Plates clinked around her. "You might remember Natalie, she used to work here, but now she runs the bookstore."

She figured Maisey was clearing the dirty dishes from the table, and by the sound of them, they were stacked high.

How many pieces of pie did I eat?

"That's wonderful."

"It is, but me talking about the happenings in town won't help your situation. I'd bring you home to our place, but our spare room only has a toddler bed for Sahara. You're a tiny thing, but not that small."

"Is there anyone who can give me a ride to my studio?" Maisey was silent, so much so that Sosie thought she might have left. "Are you still here?"

"Yep, still here, but it's getting dark outside. I don't think it's safe for you to be there alone."

"I'm blind, and for me, it's dark all the time." A shudder pushed through her. She'd always hated the dark. It was one of the worst things about her condition.

"I'm so sorry."

"It's okay. I'll learn to deal with it." Life was handing her an extra helping of trial and error. She had no idea what she would do, but she couldn't worry about being blind when there was a bigger problem at hand—she was stuck.

She wanted to laugh at herself. Since when did becoming blind become the lesser evil in her life? Since her agent abandoned her, and she had no place to stay for the night. It was funny how perspective played such a huge role in people's lives.

At this moment, her only option was to get to her studio. At least there, she'd be inside. She could crank up the heat and stay the night if need be. It wasn't ideal, but it was something.

"Staying in my studio is my only option at this point." She reached inside her purse and pulled out two twenties. "Can I pay my bill?"

There was a moment of silence. "How do you know what is what?" Maisey asked. "I mean, how do you know those are twenties?"

Sosie had asked the same question not too long ago.

"I fold them differently, and I carry nothing over a twenty."

She unfolded the bill, which was a quarter of its original size. "Twenties get folded in half twice, once by length and once by width. Tens get a single fold by length. Fives get folded once by width. Ones stayed the same. Coins are easy since they feel different."

"Fascinating. That makes sense, but how do you know initially what they are?"

"I have to trust that the people around me have my best interests at heart."

"Well, we do." Maisey pressed the twenties back into her palm. "Today's meal is on me—a welcome back gift. As for the ride, let me see what I can do. You can sit tight or stretch your legs." She stalled for a second. "Do you use one of those canes?"

"I do." Sosie reached into her bag and took out her white cane. With a flick of her wrist, she could turn it from folded to ready to use. "I'm not very good with it. I've been known to clobber a few ankles."

Maisey laughed. "I'd say if someone doesn't move out of your way, then they deserve a good hobbling."

"Deserve it or not, if they don't move, they'll most likely get a whack, regardless." She shifted out of the booth and swung her purse to her shoulder. "Thanks for everything. I'm going to try my hand at finding my way around town. Send out Search and Rescue if I disappear." She hoped she sound lighthearted, but inside, she felt anything but. She sucked at maneuvering through life. If LightHouse gave a grade on handling her blindness, she would have failed. She was terrified of venturing out by herself but sitting in a booth until someone rescued her wasn't a viable option.

"Let me work on a place for you to stay, at least for the night. You're not sleeping in your studio. Give me an hour and then meet me in the Brewhouse."

Sosie pulled her lip between her teeth. "The Brewhouse is

across the street, right?" She never spent much time in town when she came for a visit. She stayed at B's Bed and Breakfast, ate at the diner, and spent her days painting in the studio. She couldn't recall once going to the bar.

"Yep. Just follow the scent of hops. That will either be the Brewhouse or Zachariah."

"Who's Zachariah?"

"He's the local bootlegger and often smells like mash, which, to me, smells more like he hasn't bathed in weeks."

The bell above the door rang. "Brewhouse in an hour," Maisey said, then rushed off to greet the new patrons. "Your booth is empty Doc, will it be apple or cherry pie today?"

Sosie extended her cane and tried to remember her mobility training: walk right, tap left. She swung the walking stick in an arc in front of her.

In her head, she heard her counselor's voice: "Echolocation will be your friend."

"Friend my ass." She banged into a few empty chairs until she found a clear path. She stopped and took in the sounds around her. To her left, ice cubes dropped from the soda machine, which meant the front door was to her right, so she moved in that direction. The sound of the cane was supposed to change as she neared walls and barriers, but she never heard the difference. Maybe she hadn't paid close enough attention. Her orientation and mobility training at LightHouse happened in a city where noise surrounded her. Perhaps she hadn't honed those skills yet.

She moved her cane from left to right repeatedly, tapping the tiled floor until she met resistance. She slid it vertically along the door until she came to the handle and exited.

Outside, the cool mountain air hit her with reality. She was alone, in a small town, and didn't have a clue as to what she would do.

She found a space against the wall and dug her phone from her purse. "Hey, Siri, call Theresa." It was the third time she'd tried that afternoon, but her agent hadn't answered.

It rang twice before Theresa picked up.

"I'm not coming to get you."

Emotions roiled in her stomach while bile rose in her throat to choke her.

"You left me sitting in a diner. I have no place to go."

"Not my problem. Add it to the list of yours. You owe the Albright's thirty grand, and you owe me a dozen paintings for the exhibit, but I'll settle for ten."

"Oh my God, are you going to leave me here?"

"I already did. I'm back in Denver. Where are you?"

She turned around in a circle. "I have no idea."

"Figure it out, sweetheart, life won't wait for you to join it. I'll need those canvases shipped to my office within the month."

"You know I can't do that." She gripped her cane so hard her knuckles hurt. "How am I supposed to paint when I can't even find the studio?"

"Swallow that pride and ask for help."

"I'm asking you." Her voice quivered.

"I'm done helping. Isn't it time you helped yourself?"

Before she could say another word, Theresa hung up.

Sosie stood in stunned silence because she had no one to turn to. She moved her cane left to right and walked aimlessly down the street until she hit the drop off at the curb. She took a deep breath and focused her attention on what she heard. Except for the chirp of birds and an echo of laughter, there was nothing.

To step off the curb was like free-falling into the unknown. There could be a car coming, and she wouldn't see it barreling toward her. Logic said she would hear it, but what about a Prius? Those cars were virtually silent.

"Screw it." She stepped off the curb and moved into the street. Dying wasn't the worst thing that could happen; going blind was. Losing her sight caused her to lose everything. If she wasn't an artist, who was she?

CHAPTER FOUR

"Welcome to Aspen Cove," Baxter walked into Merrick Buchanan's home on Rose Lane. Baxter looked at the house months ago before he purchased his, but it was out of his budget. However, he was familiar with what it lacked and what it needed.

"Thanks, it's a huge change from the city, but a welcome respite from the craziness."

Baxter laughed. "Oh, we've got our own brand of crazy. Generally, it comes in the form of gossip, but at least that doesn't kill you."

"I can handle gossip, but dodging bullets, I can do without."

Baxter moved into the kitchen, where the bulk of the work was needed. "Not much of that happening here until hunting season. There's always some jackass who gets careless, but no one has been shot." Baxter chuckled. "Take that back. There was one guy who shot himself in the foot."

"Idiot."

"That's what Doc said. He patched him up and told him fishing was less painful." He leaned against the kitchen counter.

"Tell me what you want to do." His foot moved over the missing floor tile.

Both of their eyes went to the space where the wood subfloor showed through.

"New floor for sure. You probably need to make sure the subfloor isn't rotting through."

"It isn't. I looked at this house before I bought mine."

Merrick's eyes grew wide. "What turned you off from this one?"

"The price."

"Ah." He nodded. "It's all relative, I guess. Put this house in Littleton, and it would cost me three times as much and would probably be in worse condition. Since you know the house, why don't you tell me what you think needs to be done."

This is where Baxter shined because he had a good imagination. "Obviously, the floor is a problem. If it were mine, I'd tear this tile out and put down hardwood to match the rest of the house. The problem with these older homes is that they are compartmentalized. You can't really see the beauty of them at a single glance. Having said that, if you're tearing up the floor, I'd also remove this wall." He shoved off the counter and walked straight ahead to tap the wall dividing the kitchen from the living room. It's not true to the era, but it would open up the place and make it user friendly.

Merrick rubbed his clean-shaven jaw.

Baxter didn't understand how, at after six in the evening, he didn't have at least a shadow. A quick touch to his own jaw showed he was well on his way to a beard or would be by the end of the day. The hair on his head grew about an inch a month, but the stuff on his face seemed to sprout a quarter inch a day.

"I'm not sure a teardown is in the cards for me. Wes gave me an allowance for tile, paint, trim, and fixtures."

Though Baxter thought dismantling the house was a good

idea, it would mean he'd have to spend more time on the project. However, more time here meant less time at his own home, so he didn't press the issue.

"Okay, so let's tear up the floor and install hardwood. If I refinish the rest of the floors at the same time, I can get a good match. If you want to keep it simple, let's do white subway tiles on the backsplash. I'm sure I can talk Wes into a granite slab for the countertops, so you don't have grout lines. There's a fine line between paying respect to the house as it was and how it actually should be. A certain amount of luxury is expected in a home these days."

Merrick nodded. "Great, what about the bathroom? Is there a way to raise the height of the showerhead?"

Laughter rolled through Baxter. "Yep, I would have done the same. They made these homes for less imposing people. How tall are you?" He was a decent height at nearly six feet, but Merrick was a giant.

"I'm six-six."

Baxter looked around him. "It's a good thing this place has nine-foot ceilings." They moved to the bathroom, where Baxter swept the shower curtain back and looked at the plumbing fixtures. "Rainshower, pulse, or regular."

"What?"

"What type of showerhead do you want?"

"Oh, umm ... how about regular? I'm a simple guy."

"Regular it is." There was nothing regular going on in the shower at his home. He put an adjustable showerhead in that could pound and pulse his flesh with hot steamy water. Who needed a masseuse when he had one of those?

"I'd like to keep the lighting fixtures the same. I kind of like them." He walked into a nearby bedroom. All that hung from the ceiling were wires. "Any way you can find a matching light for this room?"

"Yep." He had a few at his house. He also liked the bubble

glass and bought several when Mason Van der Veen gutted a few houses in town.

Merrick looked at him. "When can you get started?"

"I've got quite a bit on my plate right now, but it won't take me long once I begin. We're talking mostly cosmetic stuff. How about next week?" He knew Wes wanted him to start on the band members' homes, but he figured he could do a few days on each project and save the weekends for his place. That way, everyone got what they needed.

"Okay, Monday, then?"

"I'll be here at six."

Merrick groaned and pulled his keys from his pocket. "I'm still clearing things out in Denver." He looked around the empty house. "Take the key and come and go as you please. I'm not moving up until the place is ready."

Baxter pocketed the key. He hadn't considered Merrick would have to travel from Denver. With no one to inconvenience him or work around, he might be able to finish earlier if he worked nights too.

The men walked to the front door. Baxter stepped outside and turned around. "I'm heading to Bishop's Brewhouse. If you're interested in a beer, I'll buy the first round."

Merrick nodded. "I could use a beer. Just one, though, because I have a long-ass drive back to Denver."

They both climbed into their vehicles and headed into town. He beat Merrick by a car length. Both parked side by side down the street and walked together toward Bishop's Brewhouse.

"What's the female situation here in town?" Merrick asked.

Baxter pulled the bar door open. "Single women in Aspen Cove are like unicorns. If you find one, it's a rare thing."

They walked inside the bar and slid through the crowd surrounding the pool table.

"Is this normal for a Wednesday night? Seems busy for such a small town."

"It's hump day, and that means two for one happy hour." He glanced down at his phone. "We've got fifteen minutes to fill up on cheap booze."

"I told you, I'm only good for one. I've got a three-hour drive ahead of me."

Baxter moved toward the bar and stopped when he saw Sosie sitting on the end stool, sipping a glass of white wine. She looked around the room as if she could see everyone in front of her.

"Who's the hottie at the end," Merrick asked.

Baxter laid a twenty on the bar and asked Merrick what he wanted.

"The blonde and a Budweiser."

"Listen, man, she's not for you."

"How do you know?"

"First off, she doesn't live here. Second, she's ..." Was it his story to tell?

"She's what?"

"Blind."

Merrick's brows lifted, but a smile crossed his face. "When the lights are off and we are wrapped between the sheets, no one needs to see. You can feel your way."

"No, man. I'm asking you to leave her alone. I don't think she would be a good fit." He didn't know why, but he had this profound need to look out for her. It was ridiculous because, as a protector, he was a downright failure.

The force Merrick used to pat Baxter's shoulder sent him into the bar. "Dude, you're sweet on her."

"No way. Not interested at all." He nodded to Cannon, who pulled beers from the taps behind the counter. "Give me two Budweisers."

Cannon filled the frosted mugs and slid them across the

bar. "Doc wants to see you." He jutted his chin toward the crowd.

Baxter looked from side to side and then behind him, searching for the old man. He pointed to himself. "Me or Merrick?"

"You." He nodded to the corner. "He's over there with Katie." Cannon wiped his hand on a bar towel and offered it to Merrick to shake. "So, you're Merrick? Welcome to town. When do you start?"

Baxter looked at Sosie and then at Doc. He considered saying hello to her, but Doc waved him over. As he passed Merrick, he said, "Not for you, man. I'm serious."

"Got it. She's yours." Merrick said.

"No." He shook his and decided it wasn't worth saying again. As he moved toward Doc's table, Katie rose and headed to the bar.

Doc pointed to one of the three empty seats. "Please, sit down, son. I need to ask a favor of you."

He took the empty chair across from Doc. "What can I do for you, sir?" He had a lot of respect for the father figure of Aspen Cove. While he'd never had lengthy conversations with him, he could see why everyone loved the old man with the gruff exterior but a heart soft as a marshmallow.

"You know, here in Aspen Cove, we take care of our own." Doc sipped his beer, leaving foam on his bushy white mustache. "Defining our own is simple; if you're here, then you're family."

Baxter didn't know what Doc referred to. "I'm sorry, sir, but you've lost me."

"I need you to open up your place to someone for a bit." He shook his head. "Don't say no just yet. You're living in the only place that has an available room that's free of charge. Seems to me that since Katie has been kind enough to let you live in the apartment above the bakery, you can help me out here."

"Of course." He wasn't used to having a roommate, but he couldn't argue with the facts. He didn't pay rent, so he couldn't make the rules. "When do you need the room?"

"Tonight."

He'd have to go home and tidy up the place. Not that he was a slob, but there were dishes in the sink, and he'd thrown a shirt or two about the living room. "No problem. Just send him over when he gets into town."

"She's already here." Doc looked beyond him.

Baxter twisted his head to look over his shoulder. Behind him stood Katie, who guided Sosie to the table. His heart took off like a racehorse out of the gate.

"Not her."

Doc cocked his head. "What's wrong with her?"

"She's blind."

"Blind, yes. Deaf, no," Sosie said from behind him. She turned toward Katie. "This is a bad idea."

"Sit." Doc pointed to another empty seat, but Sosie continued to stand until Katie lead her to the chair.

Baxter leaned in and whispered to Doc, "I'm not good at babysitting."

Sosie sat up. "I haven't needed a sitter since I was ten."

He gave Doc a pleading look. "I'm a bad caretaker. The last thing I was responsible for died."

"What was it?" Doc asked.

"A goldfish I got at the fair."

"You're lucky it lived until you got it home."

Baxter shook his head. "That's not the point. The point is I suck at taking care of people."

"No one is asking you to take care of her. All she needs is a place to sleep for a few days."

"But she's blind, and the apartment is on the second floor. There are stairs."

Doc grumbled something about puppy brains. "There's nothing wrong with her legs or her mind."

"How is she going to know when she's at the top or the bottom?"

Doc turned to face Sosie, "Can you count, Sosie?"

"Forget it." Sosie rose from her seat, but Doc reached out and took her arm, tugging her back to the chair.

"Nope, it's settled. Baxter will take you over when you're ready." Doc rose from his seat. "My work is done here." He stood and looked at Baxter. "You've got the beer since you've been a pain in my keister." He turned toward Sosie. "I'd say you're entitled to another glass of wine because of his insensitive nature."

She picked up her wineglass and brought it to her lips. "I'll take a chardonnay, please. Lord knows I'll need it."

Katie put a key in Sosie's hand. "You can stay as long as you want. The apartment over the bakery is kind of a community hostel—a stopping point on the road to something more permanent."

"Thank you." She looked at Katie with gratefulness.

How was it that her eyes could be so damn beautiful and expressive?

"I'll be right back." Baxter rose and moved toward the bar. When he got there, he ordered two beers for himself and two wines for Sosie. Something told him they'd need them.

Cannon put the drinks on a tray and nodded toward the table. "Who's the woman?"

"Sosie, the artist chick, and apparently she's my new roommate."

"Sucker." Cannon laughed. "Doc's fixing you up."

He hadn't considered that a possibility and doubted the probability. "Nope, it's just Doc taking care of his own."

"She is easy on the eyes if you know what I'm saying."

"That's part of the problem, she may look, but she isn't

seeing a thing." He moved through the crowd with the tray and set it down on the table.

He put both glasses of wine in front of her. "Wine at twelve o'clock."

She slid her hand forward until her finger brushed the stems of the glasses. "Two? I need two?"

"I know I do, and I didn't want you rushing me."

She turned toward him. "As soon as I clean out my studio, I'm gone."

"How do you propose to do that? Do you have a system? Forgive me for my insensitivity, or maybe I'm stupid, but if you can't see anything, how will you pack it up?"

She twisted her lips. "I'll need help, but I'll figure it out."

"I won't be much use to you."

She waved her hand in the air. "I've heard. You're not good at taking care of things."

He drank his first beer without so much as a breath between gulps. "It's important to know your weaknesses."

"Or your strengths. I've got a skilled bullshit meter, and it's been going off since I met you."

CHAPTER FIVE

Sosie sat in her chair sipping Chardonnay and listening to the surrounding conversations. If she could see, she would have sworn the light changed and a dark cloud hovered over their table.

"Care to introduce me to your girl?" A deep voice sounded from her left.

She had no idea what her facial expression implied, but hoped it was shock and surprise.

"His girl?" She laughed. "First of all, I'm thirty, so I'm a woman. Second, I belong to no one." She picked up her glass of wine and emptied it, then moved to the second glass. "Who are you?"

The air shifted around her, and the scent of spicy cologne burned her nostrils. The seat to her right scraped against the floor when someone pulled it out, and whoever stood to her left, now sat on her right.

"I'm Merrick Buchanan. I'm new in town."

She twisted in her seat to follow his voice. "Hello, Merrick. I'm Sosie Grant, and I'm not interested."

He chuckled. "I can see that. Just wanted to stop by and say hello." There was a lull in the conversation. "You're right, man, she's not for me. I prefer my women to be kind of heart and spirit, but hey, if you like them prickly, good on you."

Her jaw dropped open, but no words came out. After the grinding of chair legs against the floor, the air shifted again, and she knew he had left.

"Did you tell him I was your girlfriend?"

"Hell no. I have no use for a girlfriend."

The strain caused by the narrowed eye expression made her forehead ache. "No use? What an asshole."

"That's the second time you've called me that. You're entitled to your opinion, but you'd be hard-pressed to find anyone else in town to call me that. I have three rules in my life."

She held up her hand to interrupt him. "Let me guess. Don't shop when you're hungry, don't date when you're horny, and don't update your status when you're drunk?"

"You are prickly, but you're wrong. My rules are, be kind to others, keep your promises, and speak the truth."

"Okay, let's test your rules. Are you angry because you're forced to take me in?"

"No," he said far too fast. "Not angry. I'm inconvenienced, annoyed, maybe even a bit put out, but anger isn't an emotion I waste a lot of time on. It's useless to be mad."

"Beep Beep Beep Beep Beep, my bullshit meter is going off."

"Then it's defective because my thoughts on anger are this. It solves nothing, builds nothing, and destroys everything. Anger is one letter away from danger."

"Oh, he spells," she said with a hint of sarcasm.

"He sits and dances too. He also needs to get up early for work, so drink up, it's time to go if you want me to take you to the apartment."

She felt bad for being flippant with him. She wasn't normally so insolent, but losing her eyesight made her a lot more than blind. She was lost and sad and scared, and yes ... angry.

She drank the second glass of wine and stood. The room seemed to sway with the music playing on the jukebox. "Uh oh," she gripped the table and held on. "I only had two glasses of wine, but I think I'm drunk."

He moved toward her to steady her with his hands on her shoulders. "You had two with me, but how many did you have before I showed up?"

"Oh, right." She raised her hand and lifted one finger and then two. "I'm definitely drunk."

He groaned. "I don't know how this works. Can you walk? Do I need to carry you?"

She gripped his arm and moved her hand up to touch his bicep. "With these muscles, you probably could carry me."

"I know I could. You don't weigh more than a bag of cement."

She stepped back but lost her balance and fell forward into his arms. "How much does a bag of cement weigh?"

"Ninety-four pounds."

"Well, I weigh more, but I'm probably easier to handle."

"I doubt that. Shall we go?"

She lifted her purse to her shoulder and gripped his arm above his elbow. "Take me to bed or lose me forever," she said.

"*Top Gun* fan, huh?"

"Loved that movie."

He moved her through the crowd and out the door.

"Let's get you into the apartment and into bed by yourself."

They walked down the street to the end of the block, turned right twice, and stopped. She could feel the uneven asphalt beneath her feet. The gravelly edges poked into the bottom of the soft soles of her tennis shoes.

"The door to the building is the first one on your right.

Unlock it and head straight upstairs where there's a second door at the top landing. That's the apartment door."

She leaned into him. "Thanks for being my wingman."

"You got it, Goose." He counted the steps out loud as they walked up them. "Looks like fourteen."

"I can do fourteen."

"Glad to hear it."

She heard the key slip into the lock, and the hinges squeak as the door swung open. He guided her inside and closed the door.

She breathed deeply. "What's that smell?"

His body stiffened under her touch. "What smell?"

"It's like heaven. There's something sweet in the air like cinnamon and sugar."

The tenseness disappeared. "We're above the bakery. Just wait until morning when they bake the first batch of muffins. It's almost torturous."

Her stomach growled loudly, and she dropped her hands to her belly. "Shhh," she said.

"Are you hungry?"

Her head nodded, even though she said, "No, I'm fine." Her lie was drowned out by another loud grumble.

"Liar."

She hung her head and frowned. "I don't normally lie, but I also don't want to be a problem."

He put her hand back on his arm. Her fingers skated across a plush surface as they moved forward. When she turned to look at what she was touching, she swore the color blue danced past her eyes.

"You're not a problem, just an—"

"Inconvenience. I know, and I'm sorry. I'm in a bit of a pickle." She giggled.

He pulled out a chair and helped her into it. "I haven't heard that saying in a while."

"It's stupid, right? I mean, who says things like that?"

"Apparently, you do."

She heard him moving around the room, opening and closing cupboards.

"You have a few choices. I've got peanut butter and jelly, or I can make you toast and eggs, or there's Cap'n Crunch cereal."

She considered her options. "Peanut butter and jelly, please. Do you have any idea how long it's been since I've had that?" She bounced up and down in her chair like a kid.

"No idea, but by your exuberance, I'd say it's been a while. Do you want strawberry or grape jelly?"

She licked her lips like she was tasting both. "Can I have half and half?"

He let out a huff, but she could tell he wasn't all that put out. "You're a pain in my ass."

"Just wait until tomorrow when I have a headache, and I'm crabby."

"I won't be here to notice."

Her reality hit her like a brick to the head. "Right." She gnawed on her lower lip. "Does anyone drive for Uber or Lyft here?"

"Nope."

"If I had a car, that would be a great side job."

He set the plate down in front of her with a thunk. "I'd say it would be a tough sell for you."

"Haha, blind jokes. You're a real comedian."

"No, you are if you think anyone would get in a car with a blind driver." He moved away, and the cold air whooshed past her when he opened the refrigerator. "How about a glass of milk?"

"I'd love one."

"Milk at three o'clock." He put a glass to the right of her plate and sat across from her. She didn't know if he had a sandwich, too, because the room was silent.

"How do you do it?" he asked.

"Do what?" She took a bite of her sandwich and hummed. It might have been the best thing she'd eaten in all her life.

"Be blind?"

She swallowed and took a drink. "It's not like I had a choice."

"Was it all at once or gradual?"

She considered the question. "I'd like to say it happened all at once, but there were signs I ignored. My vision got blurry, but I was working night and day on a project, and I put it off as fatigue. It was a perfect storm."

He cleared his throat. "I heard you talking to your agent."

"You mean you listened, as in eavesdropped?" Talk of her condition had a way of sobering her up fast.

"I did. Not much happens around town that's all that exciting, and your story intrigues me."

"There isn't really a story. I was painting in the woods and got a tick bite. Turns out, the beast had Lyme disease. I got sick and tired, and the rest is history. I ended up with optic neuritis, which should have been temporary, but even with steroids and antibiotics, nothing returned to normal. After four months, the doctors said it was probably permanent."

"Probably? That means there's a chance it's not, right?"

She shrugged. "I held on to hope, but it seems like the world is fresh out of miracles for me." Her stomach twisted, and she was no longer hungry, but she ate the sandwich, anyway. Since Baxter had reluctantly helped her, she wasn't going to do anything to jeopardize her current reprieve.

"I heard Theresa say you were in the hospital or a facility of some type."

She laughed. "Don't worry, I'm not crazy. I was hospitalized for the Lyme disease, and then when it was obvious I would stay blind, I went to San Francisco to LightHouse. It's a program that helps with O and M or orientation and mobility.

They taught me how to walk with a cane and use my other senses to compensate for the loss."

"You seem to do okay."

"I suck at it, but I'm sure as time passes, I'll get better. I'm behind the curve because I was in denial but being left behind to figure it out is an eye-opener."

"Looks like you figured it out."

She shook her head. She had figured nothing out. "No, I just got lucky that Maisey took pity on me and found me a place to stay."

"She's a good woman. She's my aunt, and she's had a tough life too, so when she can make someone else's easier, she does."

Sosie hadn't put it all together, but it made sense. Dalton was Maisey's son, and his last name was Black. Baxter and Riley were Blacks.

"I don't know why I didn't put the pieces together."

"It's not like you don't have anything else on your mind."

She covered her mouth and yawned. "I should get to bed. I've got a busy day ahead of me, and it's full of uncertainty." She picked up her empty plate and glass. "Just guide me in the sink's direction, and I'll wash my dishes."

He took them from her hands. "I've got these. There's an entire sink filled with other dishes." She heard him set the dishes down as he said, "Let me show you to your room."

He placed her hand on his arm and walked her out of the kitchen and down what she thought was a hall. "This first room on the right is yours." He walked forward a few more feet. "The bathroom sits between our bedrooms. I'm at the end of the hallway."

She reached out and touched the doorframe leading into the bathroom. "Do you happen to have a T-shirt I can borrow to sleep in?" She stared down at her clothes out of habit. She couldn't see anything, but it didn't stop her from looking. "This is all I've got. I clearly didn't think this was how my day would turn out. We were supposed to pack up the canvases and leave, but as you know, that didn't quite happen."

"Stay here for a minute." Baxter left and was back before she could wonder where he'd gone. "Here's a T-shirt and a pair of clean boxers if you want them. My sister used to steal my clothes to sleep in and said they were comfy." He pressed them into her free hand. "Do you want to change in the bathroom, and I'll wait here to guide you to your bed?"

It almost seemed comical. She'd thought about the last time she spent the night with a man. She wasn't sure it would ever happen again, but even in her dreams, it didn't start with a "hell no" and end with his T-shirt and underwear tucked under her arm.

"If you don't mind, that would be good."

"Sink is about six feet ahead and to your right. The shower is directly across from it." He brushed past her, and she heard the toilet seat closing. "If you need to use the toilet, it's in the alcove next to the shower. I've put the seat down, so you won't fall in."

He walked beside her, and she grabbed his arm, stopping him mid retreat.

"Thank you so much for being kind."

"It costs nothing to be nice." He touched her arm. "Oh, there's toothpaste in the right-hand drawer. We can get a toothbrush tomorrow from the corner store, but for now, you'll have to be creative."

He walked out and shut the door behind him. She stood in the center of the bathroom for several seconds before she moved to the sink. Everything was exactly where he said. She did her best to brush her teeth with her finger and toothpaste. She washed her face and changed into his clothes. She swam in the shirt and had to roll the waistband of the boxers several times so they wouldn't fall to the floor. Once she folded her clothes, she opened the door and waited.

"Are you here?"

"I am." He stepped forward. "Is it okay that I place your arm on mine? I think I saw it in a movie once, and so I just assumed, but I shouldn't have."

She smelled his cologne. It was a heady mix of citrus and amber—a scent she always loved.

"That's perfect. It puts me in control. To grab me and pull me is not good."

"Okay." He once again placed her hand on his arm and led her to the spare room. "This is yours. There's a queen bed in the center of the room. It has nightstands on each side. Off to the right is a dresser, but I don't know if there's anything in there." He moved her to the bed.

When she felt the mattress hit her knees, she turned and sat down, and then stood up. "I need my purse so I can plug in my phone."

"Got it." He left the room and returned with her bag. When she pulled out her phone and charger, he plugged it in and set it on the nightstand. "Okay, is there anything else I can get you?"

She shook her head. "No, I'm fine." She was anything but fine. Her life was caught in a cyclone of despair, and she couldn't escape the spin.

His lips touched the top of her head. The kind gesture almost undid her.

"Good night, Sosie. I hope tomorrow is better for you than today." His footsteps echoed in the room, and the last thing she heard was the click of the light switch.

She was back in the dark. It was silly, but knowing the light was on comforted her.

Any relief she had was now gone. She was alone in a stranger's house with little to no options. The reality of her dire situation brought tears to her eyes, and she pulled back the covers, climbed between the sheets, and cried.

CHAPTER SIX

Baxter woke with a start, knowing something wasn't right. It could have been that he didn't get much sleep because he listened to Sosie whimper all night, and his nerves were on edge.

He flew out of bed at the scent of bacon. He didn't bother to pull on pants, just rushed to the kitchen to make sure she wasn't burning the house down.

"What the hell?"

She spun around, holding a spatula in her hand. He took her in from the top of her messy hair to the tips of her pink toenails.

"Good morning, Baxter." She moved her hand along the counter until she stood in front of the coffeepot. Two cups sat in front. "Would you like coffee?"

He stared at her for a minute, wondering if he hadn't woken up, and this was part of a dream. When the grease popped in the pan, and she jumped back, he knew he was awake.

"Give me that before you hurt yourself." He reached for the spatula. As his fingers touched the handle, she pulled it away. "I'm perfectly capable of cooking breakfast. There is no guarantee it's edible, but I'm trying." She wrapped her hand around one coffee mug and poured. Just as it neared the top, she stopped and did the same for the other cup.

"How are you doing that?"

She giggled. "I'd like to say it was practice that let me perfect my cooking, but I've only done this once before as a blind person. I'm hoping my success rate improves, given that I started the kitchen on fire the last time." She turned her head toward him and smiled. "Just kidding." She moved to the pan and flipped the bacon. "No, I'm not. I did start a fire, but it was because I let my shirt get too close to the flame."

"Did you get hurt?"

"Just my pride, but if you listen to my agent, she'd tell you I have plenty to spare. Don't let her fool you, though. I'm more of a fake it until you make it kind of girl." She pointed to the table. "Have a seat."

"I'll be right back. I need to get dressed. Promise you won't burn the place down while I'm gone?"

"Are you naked?" Her eyes opened wide.

"Umm, back in a second." As he turned around, he heard her say something about him being a sight to see.

Once he pulled on jeans and a T-shirt, he moved back toward the kitchen. When he got to the table, his breakfast was sitting there waiting. He had to give her credit because it looked damn good.

"Thank you, Sosie. You didn't have to make me breakfast."

She felt her way to the other side of the small table. "I know, but it would have been rude for me to cook for myself and not feed you. Especially since you made me a sandwich last night, and it's your food."

He was reticent to bring it up, but he had to make sure she was okay. "I heard you crying last night. I didn't want to intrude, but are you okay?"

Her cheeks pinked. "I'm sorry. It's silly really but,"—she

rolled her beautiful eyes,—"believe it or not, I'm afraid of the dark."

He dropped his fork. "Wait. What?"

"I know, it's crazy, but I've always hated the night, and now I live in a world of darkness." She stabbed a forkful of scrambled eggs and took a bite. "Not bad," she said after she swallowed. "I cooked them in the bacon grease because I couldn't find the oil."

"I usually use butter."

She nodded. "Hence no oil. That makes sense."

They sat there for a moment in silence while they ate. He looked around the kitchen. She'd cleaned the dishes and put them away. It baffled him at how he'd misread her.

"I think I owe you an apology."

She laughed. "Wait until you're certain you don't get sick."

She was funny. Despite her circumstances, she found humor in things, or at least she liked to yank his chain.

"No, I'm sorry for thinking I'd have to babysit you." The bacon he picked up was crispier than he liked but edible by any standards. "It looks like you're babysitting me."

Her hand went to her coffee cup, and she pulled the mug to her lips. She drank deeply and stared at him like she could see him. It was the most off-putting thing. Her eyes seemed to take in everything, and yet he knew she saw nothing.

"It's easy to misjudge a person until you know them."

He agreed judgment came fast and easy to most. He never thought he was like the rest of the world, but she'd proven he was. "Tell you what. Once you're dressed, I'll take you to your studio. That way, you can start packing. I have some clients to see, and then I'll stop by at lunch and pick you up."

"Really?"

"Yes, really. You found your way around the kitchen, but I don't want you trying to get to The Guild Creative Center on your own."

"I would have tried." She picked up her phone sitting next to her plate. "This is my lifeline. I could have asked it to navigate for me."

"I don't even want to think about it." He rose and put his empty plate in the sink. "It might get you there, but it won't tell you what's in your path."

"I have my cane for that."

"Are you good with it?"

She laughed. "No, I suck, but isn't it time to figure it out and get better?"

He narrowed his eyes and took her in. He wanted to dislike her because that would make his growing attraction easier to ignore.

"Get dressed. Since you cooked, I'll clean. Can you be ready in twenty minutes?"

"I'll be there in ten."

She was as good as her word. Ten minutes later, her cane tapped along the hallway and came to a stop at the kitchen entrance.

He stared at her for a few minutes. She was wearing the same clothes she had on yesterday, but something was different. As he moved toward her, he saw it was her eyes; they were no longer clouded with confusion.

"You look nice." He moved past her to get his keys from the table.

"Thank you. I used to worry about what I looked like and now ... well, I just hope my lip gloss is on my lips."

He stared at her glistening lips for too long, wondering if the shiny pink gloss was sweet tasting.

"You look good." He noticed a piece of hair that hadn't got tucked into the hair tie. "Can I fix your hair? There's rogue section hanging loose."

She pulled the elastic out, and the blonde strands fell over her shoulders. "Have at it. You can't do worse than a blind girl."

"Hey, hair is my specialty." He ran his fingers through her soft tresses. "I helped Riley with hers when we were kids. Dad remarried after mom left, but Kathy was never really a mother. She certainly did nothing to help make Riley's life easier." He pulled her hair into a ponytail and secured the hair tie. "There, it's all contained." Before she stepped away, he leaned forward and breathed her in. "What perfume are you wearing?"

"I think it's called bacon and coffee with a spritz of lavender-scented hand sanitizer."

He wrapped his arm over her shoulder. "It's working for you."

She counted the steps as she made her way down the stairs. At the bottom, she cocked her head to the side. "Told you I could count."

Side by side, they walked around the corner to where his truck was parked, and he helped her inside.

When he climbed behind the steering wheel, he turned to her. "I totally underestimated you. I don't think there's much you can't do."

"Wrong, I can't see."

He turned the key, and the engine rumbled to life.

It took them less than ten minutes to get to her studio. When they arrived, he got out of the truck and walked her to the entrance, where she stood in front of the door and took several breaths.

"Are you okay?"

"Yes." She shook her head. "No." She stuck the key in the lock and swung the door open. "I'm not sure how this will go. It feels like a funeral."

He looked at his watch. He could spend a little time helping her if she wanted his assistance.

"Let's start this together."

"I got it. You've done enough."

"I've got time." He stepped inside her studio and took in the canvases that lined the walls. The back side of the room was all windows and light. The forest sprang up in the distance, circling a meadow of wildflowers.

She silently moved there, like a moth drawn to a flame, and leaned against the windowsill. "Stunning, right? I can still see the snow on the ground from the last time I visited." She stepped back and looked at the paintings that lined the walls. "Most of them are of that meadow during all the seasons."

He walked the circle of the big room, hypnotized by the paintings and their artistry. "They're ... remarkable," he said in awe as he looked around the room. He noticed that they were all in various stages of completion; some merely had the land and sky, but others were almost finished. "I bet you could paint with your eyes closed."

She turned around and leaned against the wall.

"I used to. It was a game to me. I'd tie a bandana over my eyes and see what I could come up with."

"And?"

"They weren't all awful."

He moved toward her and set his hands on her shoulders. "I heard that you're in a bit of a pickle."

"You know those pickles, they're hard to get out of." She leaned forward and set her head against his chest. "My life is a mess."

He wrapped his arm around her back and held her close. "Maybe, or maybe you can actually save yourself. You can still paint. Your hands aren't broken."

She tilted her head back so he could see her eyes. A single tear ran down her cheek. "I can't. It's impossible."

He chuckled. "Says the blind woman who cooked me breakfast this morning. I think you're capable of anything you put your mind to. Let's see." He looked around the studio for a blank canvas. "Let's set up a canvas, and you can try it."

She shook her head. "I can't. I have no perspective."

He tapped the top of her head. "You have everything you need right here. I truly believe that you can do anything you put your mind to. I mean, you are still an artist, so you have a handle on color and scale."

She sighed but nodded. "I used to, but I'm not sure anymore."

"Just try. What can it hurt?"

"Nothing, I suppose."

"That's the spirit."

He placed a canvas on an easel and found a table where she stored her paints. "The biggest problem I see is knowing what color you're using."

"White is the thickest."

"How do you want them set up?"

Her hands shook as she felt her way across the surface of the table. "I can't do this."

"You can. Tell me what order."

She let out a growl. "Fine, let's do them in the order of the color wheel."

He set her tubes of paint in a row from yellow, green, blue, to purple, red, and orange. He placed the white and black to each side. "Your brushes are here. There's some kind of palette and a can of linseed oil."

"Thank you." She turned in a circle. "Do you see a smock around?"

He grabbed it from a hook by the door and helped her into it. A look at his watch told him he needed to go, but he hated to leave her alone. "Are you going to be okay?"

"You dropped me off so I could pack up my stuff, not paint."

"There's nothing wrong with a little detour."

She snapped the front of the blue cotton jacket together. "You know this means I have to stay longer."

"There are worse things than having you in the apartment." He moved toward the door. "What's your dinner specialty?"

She picked up a tube of paint and squeezed a dollop onto the palette. "Takeout pizza."

"I'll be back in a few hours." He realized she was missing one thing. He found a large piece of cotton sheeting in the corner. He tore off a strip, walked back to her, and covered her eyes. "Just like old times." He kissed the top of her head and left.

All the way to the new builds the Cooper brothers were erecting, he told himself he was an idiot. If he'd just packed her stuff up, she'd be on her way by tomorrow. He reminded himself that he wasn't looking for a companion or in need of love. He lacked the qualifications to be a good anything, especially a boyfriend, particularly for a woman who needed so much more than he could give.

CHAPTER SEVEN

Sitting on the floor covered in paint and shame, caused anger to boil in her veins. Painting blindfolded was not the same as painting blind. At the end of scenario one, she could take off whatever covered her eyes and correct mistakes. In the second example, there was no save.

Having fallen from the easel, the corner of the canvas covered her thigh. She picked it up and flung it across the room. She could hear the destruction of the frame as it hit the wall.

In her mind, she'd painted the meadow from memory. Tall trees rose on the outskirts, protecting the flowers. A small rabbit scurried across the field of green grass. That was her vision, but who knew what went on the canvas. For all she knew, the rabbit's head was in the trees, and the grass was climbing the bark of the pines.

She had no perspective on anything these days. How was she supposed to finish ten canvases when she could barely match her clothes? And the Albright project would never get completed. The advance would have to be paid back, but she didn't have a plan. And how was she supposed to feel about a man who loathed having her in his home, and yet, made her feel something wonderful by being there? For a moment, she had value beyond an artist, but that wasn't real. It was a mirage in a desert of despair.

The feeling that warmed her belly that morning as he pressed his lips to her hair wasn't real. He was setting her on a path to accomplish what she came here to do. His talk of painting gave her hope, but the act showed her reality—life as she knew it was over.

She buried her face in her hands and sobbed.

"I'm back," she heard from behind her.

Heavy footfalls moved toward her, and she cried harder.

"Oh hell. What happened?" Baxter knelt beside her.

The iciness of the cement seeped through her pores until she shook. The cold floor had chilled her entire being, but the heat emanating from him comforted her. She opened her mouth to speak, but a plaintive wail escaped, and she found herself being pulled into his lap. He leaned against the wall and cradled her in his arms.

Soothing words coated her while warm arms held her.

She knew she should rise and walk away, but his touch was the only thing keeping her tethered to sanity. His sweet words telling her it would be okay made it seem possible. She wanted to believe them, but she knew the truth. She was a lawsuit away from total destruction.

"I'm sorry," he whispered. "I shouldn't have left you alone." He shifted her, so she sat sideways on his lap with one arm caressing her back and the other cupping her cheek. "It's just that you were so positive this morning and ..."

She drew in a shaky breath and let her head fall against his chest. "It's not your fault. I drank the Kool-Aid because I wanted to believe my life wasn't over."

He held her tighter. "Your life isn't over, it's just different."

"I was an artist. It was how I made a living, but I'm no longer that person."

His hand rested on her sternum. "You are still an artist. It's steeped in your soul, a part of your heart, and your being."

She pointed away from them. Having nothing to give her perspective, she didn't know what she was aiming at, but it didn't matter. "I don't even know what I painted." He shifted her off his lap and rose to his feet. With his arm wrapped over her shoulders, he walked her several feet away.

"It's good, Sosie. It's not like the others, but who wants the same thing?"

"My clients."

"Get new clients."

She shifted away, but the feeling was hollow and cold, so she moved back to his side.

"What do you see when you look at the canvas?"

His body shook with laughter. "Besides the big gaping hole in the center?"

"There's a hole?"

His lips touched the top of her head again. This time they lingered there for several seconds. "Yep, it cuts straight through the forest like you were paving a road—a new road for your-self." He shifted from side to side. "I like it. What are you calling this piece?"

"Trash, I'm calling it trash. Throw it away."

His hand cupped her shoulder and pulled her closer. "No way, this is a Sosie Grant original."

"Like me, it has no value."

"I disagree. It's a progress piece, and I love it."

"You can have it. It's not even finished and never will be." She sniffled and sighed.

"Like you, it's a work in progress. None of us are ever finished. We are constantly learning and growing."

"Who are you?"

He laughed. "I'm Baxter Black, and I'm hungry. How about I take my new roommate to lunch?"

She looked up at him or at least hoped she was looking at him. "How can you eat at a time like this?"

He turned her around and unsnapped the smock. "It takes energy to recreate yourself, you'll need fuel. You're not over Sosie, your life has just begun." They started for the door when he stopped. "I almost forgot my art."

"You are not taking that, are you?"

He let her go, and the sound of his shoes moved deeper into the studio. "You gave it to me. I'd never take your gift for granted. I have the perfect place to hang it when my house is finished."

"Garage rafters?"

"Nope, this is fireplace art." He pressed his arm against her hand.

She gripped him and followed him out the door. "Perfect. Get the flame really hot and toss it in."

"Such a comedian."

"I'm serious. Just toss it away."

"Nope, let's name it."

"Rage."

She heard the car door open and a shuffling sound, then the door shut before another opened, and he helped her inside.

"I can see that, but honestly, the sun is too bright, and the bunny is too cute."

"Oh my God, you can see the rabbit?"

"Sure, it's as clear as mud." The sound of his laugh followed him around the car until he opened the driver's door and climbed inside. "If it wasn't for the ears, I wouldn't have really known."

"It's awful, isn't it?"

"Nope, it's beautiful, and you know why? It came from your

soul. That painting is the beginning of something." He put the truck in gear and pulled forward.

"That painting is wet, and you're insane."

The truck shifted, and the ground turned from bumpy to smooth.

"Wait, I forgot my bag and my cane."

He reached over and grabbed her hand. "Do you trust me?"

Did she? She had to because, at this point in her life, there was no one else to count on.

"I'm driving blind here, Baxter. I don't know what direction to go anymore."

"Go in the direction I'm going. I won't leave you behind."

"Will your direction take me by the Corner Store to get a toothbrush?"

He let go of her hand, and there was a rustling sound that came from behind. "I already got you one and some face wipes and some moisturizer my sister says a girl can't live without."

She sat in stunned silence. "Why would you do that?"

"Maybe I'm nice, or maybe that breakfast was the best meal I've eaten in a long time, and I'm jockeying for more."

"You're insane."

He made a hard left, then came to a stop. "I've been called worse. Just last night, some hot chick called me an asshole."

She knew he was referring to her. "Are you sure you should drive?"

He killed the engine. "I'm an excellent driver, why?"

"'Hot chick'? I think you might be vision impaired too."

"Come on, let's eat." He exited the car at the same time she did, although she stood next to her closed door waiting for him. He asked her to trust him, and this was his first test. She couldn't depend on anyone who led her astray.

She smelled his cologne on the air as he approached to take her hand and place it on his arm.

"What's that cologne you wear?"

He leaned in and whispered, "It's a signature blend called cocky asshole."

She smiled. "It fits you." How funny was it, that only a half an hour before she was ready to throw herself off a cliff, and now she was dining with a man that felt like heaven and smelled like trouble?

He led her into the diner and helped her into a booth. Moments later, arms wrapped around her in a hug.

"Oh my God, Sosie. It's been so long." The person speaking scooted into the booth next to her. "I'm sorry to hear about your vision loss."

She tried to put a face to the voice but couldn't and wished now that she'd taken the time to get to know people better.

"Riley, we're hungry."

Suddenly, the heat from a thousand suns warmed her. "Riley." If anyone knew how devastating her loss was, it would be a fellow artist. "It's so good to see you." She always thought that sounded weird because she saw nothing. "Well, not *see you*, but you know what I mean."

"I do." She gave her another squeeze and lifted from the booth. "I've got a meatloaf blue-plate special and a fresh cherry pie."

"I'm in," said Baxter. "What about you, Sosie? You want to live on the edge with me?"

Bubbles of laughter rose and tickled her throat. "Meatloaf is living on the edge? Geez, you need a more exciting life."

"He's a regular choir boy. You could do better," Riley said.

By the way the callouses brushed across her hand, she knew it was his that covered hers. "She *could* do better, but she's slumming this week."

Several thoughts crossed her mind. He'd touched her possessively in front of his sister and implied that she'd be here for the week.

She turned her head to where she thought Riley stood. "If

I'm staying the week, I'll need sustenance. Make that two blue-plate specials."

He squeezed her hand. "That's my girl."

"Coming right up."

"Bring two sodas as well," Baxter called after his sister. "Is soda okay with you?"

She smiled, "You're not really an asshole."

"Glad you think so."

Riley swept by and put two sodas on the table.

"Why did you tell her I'd be staying the week?"

She could hear him unwrap a straw. He pressed it into her hand. "Doc said something last night. He reminded me that in Aspen Cove, we take care of our own and you're ours Sosie. I got a look at that studio, and frankly, we'll be lucky to pack it up in a week."

The heavy weight of the task at hand pressed on her. "It doesn't really matter anymore. How Theresa thinks I will produce ten canvases for a show is beyond me." She put her straw in the drink and took a long draw. "Is there anything finished there? I really can't remember?"

"I don't think so. I'm not exactly familiar with your work, but most of them have blank sections on the canvas."

She left out a breath. "I'll get sued."

Riley dropped off their meals.

"Meatloaf at twelve, mashed potatoes at four, and green beans at six," Baxter said.

"Thank you. You're very good at this. No one's ever really clocked my food, but it's helpful."

"Looks like we're both learning. I'm really the shits at taking care of people, which was why I was reluctant to have you as a guest, but you're resilient."

She swallowed a bite of potatoes and gravy. "Hardier than a carnival goldfish?"

"I'm sorry about that, but I have a bad track record."

She smiled. "Well, you're doing okay with me. Thankfully, I don't need a babysitter." She thought about that. "Except for today. I needed everything, including a seeing-eye human, for you to bring me to lunch, and clean underwear."

"I can help with the first two, and you're welcome to borrow my boxers to solve the third."

"I can wrap your boxers around me twice."

"You're wearing his boxers?" Riley asked.

The heat of a blush rose to Sosie's cheeks. "It's not what you think. I wasn't expecting to be stranded in Aspen Cove, and your brother was kind enough to lend me something to sleep in. Now that I'm here for a bit, I need to figure out my clothing situation." She skimmed her hands down her shirt to her jeans. "This is all I've got."

"I'm on it. If there's one thing about this town, it's that they take care of their own."

"So, I've heard."

"You look like a six. Am I close?"

"Spot on. Once I get my phone back—"she made a face at Baxter, or at least she thought she made it at Baxter, but it could have been seen by everyone,—"I'll order some things from Amazon."

"Women." Baxter shook his head. "Even the lack of sight doesn't stop you from shopping."

"No, only lack of money stops me from shopping, but good credit helps." Lord knew she had no money. All she could count on was the eight hundred dollars and change the state gave her for her disability payment each month. Really, how was a person supposed to live on less than a thousand dollars a month?

"I bet you I can have a change of clothes or two here by the time you finish your pie."

"It's okay," Sosie said. "If wearing the same clothes is the worst thing that happens to me today, then I'm doing good."

Perspective. It's all about perspective. She would be smart to remember that.

Alone again, she asked, "Tell me, Baxter, what exactly do you do?"

"I'm in construction. I do lots of things, but mostly I'm known for my finish work."

She giggled. "Now, you're bragging. Leave it to a man to boast about his ability to finish."

"What? No, I meant..."

She knew exactly when he figured out she was teasing because he moved to her side of the booth and leaned close to her ear. "You will be trouble for me, Sosie. You're the perfect mix of sassy, sweet, and sexy for my palette."

"Me? Trouble? You bet your ass." She stabbed a bite of meatloaf.

The sound of his plate sliding across the table made her smile. She scooted over to give him more room.

"What's on the agenda after lunch?" she asked, expecting him to say he was taking her back to the studio.

"We have to visit some homes. You can be my assistant." He gently shoulder checked her. "It's the least you can do since I'm buying you lunch."

"Your assistant? Doing what?"

"You're great with color. I think you can help me with the finish work."

"You're nuts."

"Maybe, but this will be fun."

"Will the client be there?"

"Owen Cooper will be."

She didn't know who that was. "Imagine how pleased he'll be when he sees you've brought a blind woman to help design his house."

Baxter clapped his hands. "I can't wait."

A few minutes later, Riley was back with pie and a bag of

clothes. "Told you I could get it done. There are a few pairs of jeans, a T-shirt, and a sundress. I failed on the underwear, so you might have to go without."

Baxter groaned. "I didn't have to know that."

His sister laughed. "Something tells me you won't mind having that vision in your head."

Sosie laughed. "I miss my brother."

"Where is he?"

She was tired of covering up for him. "Rehab. He's part of the reason I'm in such a jam."

"A pickle," Baxter added.

"I'm thinking I might like pickles if they include people like you," Sosie said.

"Cute," Riley said. "You two are cute together. Who would have thought?"

"What?" They both said together. "No."

CHAPTER EIGHT

"You want to help me play a joke on a friend?" He drove down Main Street and made a right on Lily Lane.

"Depends. Do I have to get naked and dance on a table?"

His foot hit the brake, and he came to a full stop in the middle of the street. "What? Is that a thing?"

"Could be." She giggled. "It hasn't been for me, but who knows, I'm just defining the rules before I get in too deep."

He considered her statement of getting in too deep and wondered if he'd crossed the line earlier.

"Speaking of too deep." He cleared his throat. "I may owe you an apology for earlier when I held you."

She turned to him with those big eyes. "You're apologizing for offering me comfort?"

He shook his head and then remembered that she wouldn't see his gesture. "No, I'm apologizing for not asking you if you wanted to be comforted."

She reached her hand out until she found him. Her fingers gripped his arm. "I'm grateful you saw I needed something. I wasn't sure what I needed, but you intuitively knew I needed to be held."

He let out a sigh. "I just don't want to overstep, or put you in an uncomfortable position, or make you think I'm taking advantage of your, I mean, you." He would say disability, but that sounded so harsh. Sure, she had some issues, but when he looked at Sosie, all he saw was an amazing woman.

That scared the hell out of him because he felt things for her that he had no right to feel. She was a woman who would always need extra, whether it was help, or encouragement, or possibly love. How did a person lose something as important as her sight and not need more? He wasn't the man to give that to her.

"You're safe. Besides, I enjoyed being in your arms. For the first time in a long time, I felt safe."

"I don't want you to get the wrong idea. I'd do the same for my sister."

She let her hand slip from his arm. "That makes you a good brother."

Or an asshole. He eased the truck forward and came to a stop in front of the new build. He had to give the Cooper Brothers credit; they could put up a house quickly.

"Are we here?"

"Yes." He killed the engine and sat staring straight ahead. "Look, Sosie. I like you, and I didn't mean that I thought of you as my sister. When I look at you, I don't see my sister."

When he looked at her, he saw beauty and intelligence and strength. And yes, his sister was all those things, but she never made him feel all warm inside. Thank goodness because that would be wrong.

She smiled. "When I look at you, I see nothing."

Could a heart crack? He hated that she couldn't see him. There were so many silent messages exchanged with a look.

"I'm not much to look at."

"Do you look like Riley? I mean … she's an attractive woman."

"We're twins."

"Literally?"

"Yep, but I don't look like her. I favor our father, who has darker hair and a stockier build."

"And your eyes? What color are they?"

"Brown."

"No eyes are simply brown. Give me more detail."

He pulled down the visor and looked in the mirror. "They're brown."

"Not true. What kind of brown?"

He never considered that his eyes could be considered anything else. He had to look at them through her eyes—an artist's eye.

As he took in the depths of his irises, he saw flecks of gold and onyx. The canvas of his eyes was indeed brown, but more of a reddish-brown.

"They're nutmeg with flecks of amber."

She closed her eyes as if she could see them in her mind. "Beautiful. And your hair?"

"A rich brown like dark chocolate."

"Thank you for that." She brushed her hands through her hair. "So, what's this joke we're playing?"

Now that he thought about it, it seemed ridiculous and insensitive. "Oh, nothing."

"There was something. Tell me. I have a great sense of humor, and I'd love to be in on it."

"I was going to give you a clipboard and tell him you were the designer, but in hindsight, I can see that was inconsiderate of me to use your loss as a joke."

Her lips lifted into a devilish smile. "I'm totally in. I'll need something to write on."

He reached into the back seat, where the torn painting sat, and picked up a clipboard from the floor.

"Are you sure?"

"Totally. It might be nice to find some humor in my situation. Let's take it over the top. Who is the client?"

"The builders are the Cooper brothers, but it's Owen we are meeting along with the lead guitarist from Samantha's band. His name is Gary, but he goes by Gray because Gary is far too common a name for a musician." He handed her the clipboard and a pen.

"Oh, brother."

"Are you ready?"

Her eyes sparkled. "I am. Let's hit it." She opened the door. "I'll still need your help to get inside. I'll pretend to look normal until you ask me a question, and then I'll put on the show."

He leaned over and touched her arm. "You are normal, Sosie. Never let your lack of sight, or anything else, make you feel you're not."

"I like you, Baxter, with the nutmeg eyes and dark chocolate hair." She slid out of the truck and waited for him.

I like you too, Sosie. More than I should.

He walked to her side and tucked her hand into the crook of his arm. "Let's do this."

"Is it a single story?"

"Yes, it's a rancher with an open floor concept. We'll walk into the great room, and straight ahead will be the kitchen. There's no tile or paint or trim or flooring. That's what we're here for."

"Got it."

He walked her forward and knocked on the door.

Owen opened it. "Baxter, come on in." He called over his shoulder. "Gray, Baxter is here." The thunk of shoes against the subfloor got louder as the man got closer.

"Hey man, good to see you."

Sosie smiled and held out her hand. "I'm Sosie, your interior designer."

Owen's eyes opened wide. "Wes hired an interior designer?"

"Only the best for you guys," Baxter said. "She's great with color."

"What were you thinking?" she asked.

He didn't know how she did it, but she stared straight at Gray.

"I wasn't thinking anything, so it's great to have a professional around. Let's get started."

"Do you mind if I do my thing? I'm more of an intuitive designer."

"Have at it."

She pushed the clipboard into Baxter's hands and said, "Follow me and take notes." Her hands reached out in front of her as if she was grasping for something in the dark. And, of course, she was. She touched the wall and laid her hands flat on the surface. "Feels white. Boring. How about a soft beige?"

"Beige is better than white?" Gray asked.

"Infinitely. Or we can pick a gray to go with your name. Something like a dove gray, which has a hint of blue to it. It's not enough to think it's blue, which is why it's called a gray."

"I like it."

She turned to look at Baxter but missed her mark and stared off in a different direction. "Write that down." She dropped to her knees and touched the floor.

"Tile, wood, or carpet?" She crawled across the floor on all fours until she head-butted Owen's shin. "Oops, sorry. It's a bitch to be blind."

"What the hell?" Gray said.

Baxter rushed to her side. "She's blind."

"And she's picking out the colors for my house?"

"Yes, because to tell the truth," he pulled her to her feet and wrapped his arm over her shoulder, "she is incredible with color."

"You're screwing with us, right?" Owen moved his hand in front of Sosie's face, but she didn't flinch.

"Yes, and no, she's not really the interior designer; she's a friend, and we thought we'd mess with you."

Sosie laughed. "It was his idea, but I was game." She leaned into Baxter. "In all seriousness, I think the color scheme is still good." She reached for the clipboard and pulled the pen loose. In front of them, she drew a 3D rendering of a room. Her fingers moved over the pencil lines. "The walls would look amazing in dove gray. I'd either go with a weathered wood floor in a darker gray range or tile that looks like wood. It's durable and easy to clean."

Both men looked at Baxter with wide-opened eyes, but it was Gray who spoke up. "I like it. What about the kitchen, Sosie?" He rested his hand at the small of her back and guided her forward.

Gray's hand on her filled Baxter with raging heat; he didn't like another man touching her. Even though he knew the emotion was ridiculous, it was still there.

He followed them into the kitchen, where she leaned against the cabinet.

"What would you do in here?" Owen asked, obviously intrigued by the woman in front of him. Baxter didn't worry about him, though because rumor had it, he was sweet on some lumber mill owner named Carla. Owen's interest was purely professional.

"What color are the cabinets?"

"They're a true white with cool undertones," Baxter gave Gray a smug smile. "She likes details."

It fascinated him to watch her move her fingertips over the paper and jot down notes and drawings. Her scale was nearly perfect.

"With everything monochromatic, you can do something bold in here with the countertops. Solid surface would be my choice. It's prettier, and there are no grout lines." She giggled. "I'd never be able to see them close enough to keep them clean."

"What about granite," Owen offered.

"That works, but I'd go with something that had a lot of movement to it. Pull out the grays and whites with maybe a splash of black veining."

"She's good. Tell me, Sosie, were you always blind?"

She smiled. "We are all blind to some things, but I lost my sight just six months ago." She turned toward the window and rubbed her eyes. "Your yard is beautiful. Love that big tree." She shook her head and rubbed at her eyes again.

Her comment didn't faze anyone but Baxter. He moved behind her and looked at what was out back, and to his surprise, there was an enormous oak tree.

Sosie massaged her temples and winced.

"Are you okay?" Baxter asked.

She nodded, "Just a headache. Do you mind if I sit the rest out in the truck?"

He put the clipboard on the cabinet and walked her outside. "Are you sure you're okay?"

"Yes, I'm sure. I'm probably dehydrated."

He helped her inside the cab and pulled a bottle of water from the back seat. "Did you see that big oak tree in the backyard?"

Her eyes opened wide. "No, I just assumed there would be one."

Something in her expression changed. She tilted her head in confusion and then righted herself.

"You're obviously intuitive." Against his better judgment, but not able to help himself, he pressed his lips to her forehead. "I'll be right back."

She gave him a weak smile. "I'll be here."

Baxter rushed back to the house to finish the consultation.

"That woman is amazing," Gray said. "Is she single?"

"No, she's not," he lied. There was no way he would sit back and watch Gray Stratton woo his girl.

CHAPTER NINE

The trip to the studio was silent except for the hum of the air conditioner and the tapping of Baxter's fingers on the steering wheel. The tension was thick enough to cut with a knife.

"Thanks for including me. That was fun."

The tapping stopped when the truck did. "You were amazing with the way you picked out his palette. Gray is really excited about the finish work." His inhale was sharp and followed by a half growl. "Gray wants to know if you're going to the Fourth of July concert in the park."

"Are you going?"

"I hadn't given it much thought. I should probably spend the day working. I'm already behind with my projects."

Going anywhere without Baxter just seemed wrong. How had she grown so accustomed to his presence in a day?

"I get it. I should probably work too." She opened the door. "Can you help me inside? I can take it from there, but I'm really lost without my cane." She touched her forehead, remembering her first day of O and M training when she refused to use it and walked into a wall.

"You're staying?"

"I still have to figure out what to do with the paintings. Theresa is expecting something."

"That woman can piss off." His agitation at her agent was plain to see and feel. "She abandoned you."

"She did, but maybe it was for my own good." She climbed out of the truck and stood with her hand on the hood.

It took Baxter another minute to exit and round the front to get her.

"Are you mad at me?" she asked.

He held her hand and led her to the door. "No, what would make you think that?"

"I can't see, but I still feel those elephants in the room. Especially if they're sitting in front of me. Something has changed and it bothers me."

He cupped her cheek. "I don't like seeing you mistreated." His swallow was audible as if he were trying to gulp down a large stone. "I also wasn't comfortable seeing the way Gray looked at you. He likes what he sees."

She reached up and touched his cheek. Her fingertips moved over the stubble that roughened his jawline. "Are you big brothering me?"

"Maybe." There was another hard swallow. "No, what I'm feeling for you is not brotherly."

The wings of a thousand butterflies tickled her insides. It sounded like Baxter was jealous, and that brought her joy. After her vision faded, she thought her life was over—at least her romantic life. It wasn't like she had a lot going on in that department to begin with because she didn't get out much, and, when she did, she rarely connected with anyone since her life experiences were so different. All she knew was art, and most men couldn't hold a conversation about Monet, Picasso, Van Gogh, or Warhol. They wanted to talk sports or politics, and when that failed, they wanted sex. But with Baxter, it was different, or maybe they hadn't been in each other's company long enough for it to be the same.

He stepped back and opened the door. "What do we have to do here?"

"I have to figure out what I'll do with all these paintings. I have a lot of commitments, so I can't avoid this for too long, or I'll find myself in debtor's prison."

They walked down the hallway to her studio and flipped on the light switch. Occasionally, she saw light and shadow, and a trickle of the bright overhead lights reached her retina.

"Ahh, light."

"You can see that?"

How did she explain that she thought she saw it? It was the same as the tree. There were moments where she was certain her eyes worked for a fraction of a second, but then the minute she opened them again, it was all darkness, just like now.

"I think my brain tries to tell me I'm seeing it. Since I was once a sighted person, there are a million images in my head, and they sometimes mimic real vision."

She reached for the hook on the door and took her cane from her bag. "I'll put the canvases together and see if I can hire someone to pack them up. Maybe a moving company would work. I can't really afford one, but I can't expect to be able to do this on my own."

She tip-tapped her way to the center of the studio.

"No one would expect you to do any of this. Whatever you've got going on can wait until you're ready to deal with it. Considering I found you in a puddle on the ground earlier today, I'd say you're not ready."

"Ready or not, I still owe the Albright's thirty grand and Theresa ten Sosie Grant originals. I've got until the beginning of August to figure it out."

"Great, that means you don't have to tackle it today. How about another piece of pie?"

She wasn't really in the mood to revisit her melancholia, and she wasn't in the mood for pie. "Make it an ice cream, and you've got a deal."

"Let's go, Ms. Grant, Sam's Scoops is only a short drive away."

She grabbed her bag and walked out the door. What was another day?

"What about you? Shouldn't you be working? You just said you were behind."

"I did, but somehow pulling up old wood flooring pales compared to spending the afternoon eating ice cream with you."

They were in the truck and on their way in no time. "Isn't this the place that serves ice cream with disgusting names?"

"You pegged it. I'm wondering what they'll have today. Definitely something with poop or snot."

"Gross, the thought makes me want to hurl, and yet, I'm intrigued."

"You can't pass up on dino droppings or slugs and bugs."

"Let's talk about something else. Like you. Tell me about yourself."

"Not much to tell. I'm the son of a woman who abandoned her twins and a man who drank his life away. I've got a step-mother that might make Cinderella's mom seem like a saint, although, since Riley made peace with her, she's been more pleasant."

"Parents are tough. Theresa is harping on mine all the time. She thinks my mom uses me. In fact, she's convinced that the only value I hold to my mom and brother is my ability to pay for things, but I think she's wrong."

"Do you pay for things?"

She shrugged. "Some, like rehab for my brother, and I bought my mother's house, but I wanted to do that. She had nothing left after my father left her."

"Doc says that if you don't need therapy by the time you're an adult, your parents failed."

"Well, then mine were a smashing success." She played with a string hanging from the hem of her T-shirt. "Why construction?"

Baxter never answered questions without thought. He always waited a minute, like he was considering her question. She liked that about him. It was the sign of someone who was honest. Or maybe he was taking his time to think of a lie. She hated that she couldn't see his eyes. Eyes were a window into the soul. Deep down, they always showed a person's intentions.

"I like to use my hands. I think construction should be part of the arts, too, since it's creative. Sure, it's also mathematical and science based, but I don't do that type of work. I get to do the icing on the cake stuff."

"I can see that. When I was in that house, I saw everything finished. The floor and walls and countertops were installed, and it shined. I should have asked about the style of the house, but in all honesty, I don't know the difference between a bungalow and a ranch home."

The leather seat squeaked as he moved. She imagined he sat up taller, the way she did when people talked about paints and canvases.

"Nowadays, people interchange the words, but they aren't the same. A bungalow is small and efficient, whereas a rancher has more space. Generally, they are both single story, but, often ranch-style homes in Colorado have basements."

Does Gray's house have a basement?"

"No, his is a single level ranch. It's on a nice chunk of land, so he has room to grow. The house is a green home meaning it's solar-powered and leaves a tiny carbon footprint. The Cooper's build houses from kits and can erect them in weeks."

"That's exciting. Is that the kind of house you have?"

He chuckled. "No, I have a money pit. My house is a bungalow. It's a small two-bedroom, but I've got room to grow too because the lot is huge."

"Planning for the eventual family?"

"I haven't given that much thought. Like I said, I'm not all that good at looking after people."

"Not true, you've been wonderful to me. I don't know why you'd keep telling yourself you're not good at caring for others."

"Because it's true. I um ... I should have been there when my sister was badly burned, and I should have been there when my father died in a sink full of dirty dishes."

She couldn't stop the sharp inhale because both were tragic events. "Those aren't your fault. It seems to me your father should have taken care of both of you better."

They drove over uneven ground and pulled to a stop.

"That's one way to look at it."

"It's the only way you can look at it. He was the parent, and you were his responsibility."

"True, and that's part of the reason I resist relationships. What if I suck at it like my father did?"

She unbuckled her seat belt and leaned over the center console to give him a hug. "You don't suck at it."

He remained stiff against her until she moved away. It was probably too much, too soon. She wasn't one to show affection so easily, but Baxter was as comfortable as a plush blanket. He was soft and smelled good and easy to wrap herself up in. She would have to be careful, or she could fall in love with him.

"How about that ice cream you promised me?"

They walked side by side to the truck. Birdsong and children's voices surrounded them, and the smell of damp soil mixed with waffle cones filled the air.

She bounced on the balls of her feet in anticipation. "What are my choices?"

Baxter wrapped his arm around her waist and tugged her

closer. For a man who wanted nothing to do with relationships, he seemed to always be pulling her in.

"Guts and Butts, which is chocolate ice cream with a cherry filling swirl. There's also something called Caramel and Corns, and it's basically pralines and cream. Or, there's Unicorn Poop, which has colored marshmallows and chocolate sprinkles in vanilla ice cream."

She gnawed on her lower lip deciding between option one and two. "Caramel and Corns, please."

"I thought for sure you'd choose the Unicorn Poop."

She hugged on to his arm and laid her head on his bulging bicep. "Why would I need a unicorn when I have you?"

He ordered, and she insisted on paying. Once they had their ice creams, they made their way to a table.

"Baxter?" A strange voice chimed in.

"Hey, Mercy, how are you?"

Sosie listened to the tone in the woman's voice. It was soft, like a whisper.

"I'm better now that you're here."

He scooted in so that his thighs touched Sosie's. No doubt, he was making room for the woman to sit next to him. Liking the feel of him next to her, she didn't move. Who was this Mercy woman? She leaned forward and turned her head in the right direction—she hoped. "Hello, I'm Sosie."

"Oh, are you here with Baxter?" There was a hint of disappointment in her voice.

Sosie played out the scene in her head. She could say no, which would technically be a lie because she was here with him. There was no way she could have arrived without him, but she was certain that wasn't what Mercy was asking. She wanted to know if Sosie was *with* Baxter. Thinking about him with anyone else made it hard to swallow her ice cream.

"Yes, Baxter is mine." She hardly recognized the possessive nature of her voice. "I mean, he's my ride." That put all kinds of thoughts and visions in her head. "I mean, he brought me for ice cream."

"That's so sweet." There was a pause. "Are you the artist who comes on the weekends?"

"That's me, but I haven't been here since my eyes failed me."

"That's awful. What are you going to do?"

The truth was, she didn't know.

"Sosie is helping me design the interiors of new homes. She has an eye for color." Baxter laid his hand on her thigh.

It was such an intimate gesture. How was she supposed to respond?

"But how?" Mercy asked.

"She's amazing; you should see her in action. She just designed Gray Stratton's home on Lily Lane. I'm sure Red will want her input too."

"Red?" Sosie asked. "Do they all have color names?"

"No, not Axel, his name was cool enough on its own."

Baxter leaned in. "It's really Alex. I imagine it's like a pen name. That way, fans can't find them when they're looking for downtime."

"Don't count on it. I've already seen some teenagers camped out in front of his house."

"But you live on Daisy Lane, and he's on Rose, which is totally in the opposite direction. Are you one of his fans?"

Sosie imagined if she could see Mercy, her cheeks would be colored scarlet red.

"Yes, I'm a fan, but you won't find me tucking my underwear in the chain links of his fence."

"Underwear," Sosie said out loud. "I need underwear."

"For the fence?" Mercy asked.

"No, for me." She covered Baxter's hand with hers. "Would you mind stopping someplace close so I can get a few pairs?"

"Anything for you."

"Ahh, you two are so sweet together."

Baxter stood abruptly. "We're not together."

"Really?" Mercy said with an inflection that sounded like hope.

Sosie didn't know what bothered her more, that they weren't actually together, or that Mercy was trying to home in on someone Sosie wished was her man.

CHAPTER TEN

He begged for a quick death the entire time they were underwear shopping. Watching her fondle the thin strips of cotton and lace was torture. Now that they were home, it was worse thinking about which pair she had on.

"That smells amazing." She padded down the hallway to the kitchen.

"Piper's does a great job with takeout." She moved next to him and breathed deeply. Her tongue slicked out as if to taste the air.

Why was it that his soap and shampoo smelled different on her hair and skin?

"I was thinking about your artwork."

She put her hands on his waist and moved around him to the other side. Every cell in his body ignited.

"Do we have to talk about art, right now?"

He ignored his internal desire to grab her and kiss her because that wouldn't serve anyone well.

"Yes." He put several packets of parmesan cheese and red peppers in her hand and picked up the pizza. "Let's eat in the living room. We can watch TV and talk." He wanted to palm his forehead for his stupidity. "I'm sorry. I wasn't thinking."

"No, it's okay. I watch TV with my ears now. There's a lot of shows I love."

"Let me guess, *The Bachelor* or *Gilmore Girls*." He moved with the pizza out of the kitchen and into the living room.

"No, I prefer stuff like *Game of Thrones* or *Let's Make a Deal*, but *Gilmore Girls* doesn't suck." With her finger tucked into his belt loop, she followed him into the living room.

"Couch is at nine o'clock."

"Thank you." She reached out and touched the plush fabric before she sat down. "Is the couch blue?"

He stared down at her with what he knew was confusion. "How did you know?"

Plopping down on the cushion, she said, "It feels blue."

"You are such a conundrum."

"Don't fret, I'll be out of your way before you know it."

"That's the thing." He opened the pizza box and handed her a slice. "I'm not troubled that you're here." The lie tasted sweet on his lips. It troubled him all right, but it wasn't because she was an inconvenience. Not to his life, at least, but to his senses. She tweaked everything inside him that needed a woman. Not just any woman, but her. "Anyway, I thought maybe you might want to take a break from it all. Let's take until after the Fourth of July to just breathe. Life has hit you with a lot at once, and it might be nice to have a few days where you don't have to worry."

She leaned in and shouldered him. "Ah, I think you like having me here."

"What's not to like? You cook a mean breakfast and clean dishes."

"I'm sure Mercy would love to come over and cook for you."

"Mercy? I don't know what you mean."

"Oh, please. That woman has it bad for you."

He folded his slice in half and took a bite. He hadn't ever given Mercy much thought, even though she was pretty and sweet, she wasn't really his type. She was a nurturer, and he wasn't used to having someone take care of him. He took care of himself and only himself—until Sosie. Taking care of her wasn't as much of a problem as he originally thought, and it felt good, not scary or troublesome. It was right all the way to his marrow.

"I think you're wrong. She's a single woman, living in a town where men outnumber females three to one. She can have her pick, so why would she want me?"

"Why wouldn't she?"

"One reason—I've got nothing to offer her. Besides, she not really my type."

She nibbled on the crust. In fact, she bit around the perimeter of her pizza, keeping the slice in a triangular shape as she moved about it.

"Why *Let's Make a Deal*?" Deflection was always a good choice when he didn't want to talk about things, and Mercy, or any other woman, didn't interest him.

"No changing the subject. Why not Mercy?"

His gut response was because she's not you, but he didn't say it. "I don't know. I'm not looking for anyone. I've got a lot on my plate, and fixing up my house is my number one priority. It's not that I don't like staying above the bakery, but owning a home is a big deal. What about you? Do you own a house?"

He imagined someone with her level of fame had a home—maybe two, but then again, she had made the comment that while she didn't have cash, her credit was good which meant she was probably low on funds.

"Not anymore. I used to have a loft in Denver, but I sold it when things got tight. Now I rent an apartment but might need to downsize to letting a room. Oh, how the mighty have fallen."

He finished his first slice and grabbed a second while she continued to nibble around the edge of her first.

"I would have thought you would have a sizable savings account to pull from." He hated to admit it, but he googled her, and her paintings went for thousands of dollars. The ones she did as a child could bring in hundreds of thousands.

"Poor management."

"You, or someone you hired?"

She popped the last bite of her pizza into her mouth. "It's all on me. Not that I was frivolous, but I'm a sucker for my family or anyone with a sob story. Let's just say that my mom lives in Tuscany in a villa I bought. Several families in Denver have medical insurance for the year, a few have new cars. I don't regret buying any of it, especially for my mom because she had nothing."

"What does your mom do?"

Sosie lit up. "She paints. Mostly portraits, but they're good. She always said I sucked her talent from her in the womb." She sat back and closed her eyes. "In hindsight, I believe she lived vicariously through me. I had the fame she always wanted."

That was a bitter pill to swallow because he knew how she felt. He never had a parent who truly looked out after his best interests, either. They were too consumed with themselves and their problems to pay much attention, and he imagined Sosie's mom was the same.

"Now, why *Let's Make a Deal?*"

She sat up and smiled. The same smile she did earlier that lit up the room. "Simple. It puts me on even ground. No one knows what's behind curtain number one, but I'll tell you …, statistically, it's most likely a donkey wearing a straw hat."

"Do you want a beer?"

"Sure. I'd love a beer."

"I should have served it with the pizza."

She tapped him on the shoulder. "Bad host."

Once he put the pizza away, he came back with two beers and took a seat at the other end of the couch. He flipped on the TV and scrolled through the shows. He came across a game show cable channel midway through an episode of *Let's Make a Deal.*

"This is your lucky day." He turned the volume up and sat back to watch. His eyes fell on her, and not the TV. Everything about her was beautiful, even her blindness. Because she couldn't focus on the superficial, he got to see her essence. It didn't matter that she had blue paint on the tips of her hair, or her smattering of freckles wasn't covered up to make her look like a porcelain doll. With Sosie, what he saw was what he got, and that was a breath of fresh air.

Reaching forward, he almost touched her hair when she said, "What do you think?"

He pulled his hand back and watched her child-like excitement.

"This is the big one, huh?" He refocused his attention on the television.

"Yes, how about a wager?" she asked. She pulled her feet beneath her and leaned forward.

"You want to bet something?"

She giggled. "Yes, if my curtain is worth more than yours, you buy the pancakes at Maisey's tomorrow. If I lose, they're on me."

A good bet was hard to pass up. "You're on."

"I get number three," she blurted.

He frowned. "That's hardly fair, you already told me, statistically, curtain number one has a donkey. That means I have to take number two. You've left me no options."

She shrugged. "You don't have to. Are you a betting man? If you're a risk-taker, then choose curtain one." She scrunched her nose and said, "Hee-haw, hee-haw."

"You're so funny. I think I will choose one just to prove you wrong."

She smiled. "You'll look amazing in that hat."

They leaned forward while the host made deals for curtains. No one chose number two, and when it opened, it had a car.

"Oh no, this is not boding well for either of us." She scooted closer and moved her hand up his thigh. "Where's your hand? I'm nervous."

Having her hand high on his thigh made him nervous, too. He didn't know how much more he could take before his baser instincts took over.

He clasped her hand, and they both waited for the big reveal. The host built up the suspense by teasing the contestants and offering them cash and smaller boxes. Like the contestants, they kept their curtains, hoping for the big win.

When curtain three opened to reveal a donkey wearing a straw hat, she sunk back into the cushions. "It's not possible." She laid the back of her hand on her forehead like she'd faint from disappointment. "The ass is never behind three."

Laughter bubbled up from deep inside. "Seems to me asses are found everywhere. Looks like you're buying pancakes."

She frowned like a petulant child. "Yep, looks like I am. I always deliver what I promise."

Behind his curtain were kitchen appliances, which he could have used if he got the prize.

Next, they watched the first half of *The Wizard of Oz* before they called it a night. They walked down the hallway toward their rooms, and she said, "Wouldn't it be nice if I could click my heels and make a wish?"

He stopped. "What would you wish for?" Her eyesight was his guess. It seemed like the best bet. If put in her situation, he'd wish for it.

With lips drawn into a thin line, she rocked her head back

and forth. "I'd wish for my brother to gain permanent sobriety."

Her answer floored him. "You, Ms. Sosie Grant, are a surprise." He leaned forward and kissed her cheek. "Good night."

She walked into her room and shut the door.

He spent the next hour listening to her move around, brush her teeth, and listen to her emails via voice messaging.

Finally, the apartment took on an eerie silence, but that only lasted a few minutes. At first, he heard a whimper, and then he heard her cry. She muffled it somehow, but the sound was torturous. It made his heart physically ache like a fist squeezed his organ.

Not being able to stand it any longer, he climbed out of bed and pulled on the sweatpants he kept folded on the dresser. He moved toward her room asking himself, *What the hell am I doing?*

At her door, he rapped gently and then opened it to peek inside. "Sosie, are you okay?"

She sniffled. "I'm sorry. I didn't mean to wake you. It's just that the dark sometimes gets to me."

"Can I come in?"

Backlit by the hallway light, he saw her outline. She appeared tiny and frail in the shadows of the night, curled up like a pill bug trying to protect itself.

"Yes, can you lie down with me for a few minutes?"

Kill me now. "Yes." He moved to her bed and climbed on top of the comforter. "Here, let me hold you." He reached out and tugged her close. His chin sat on the top of her head as she melted into him with her back to his front. He tightened his arms around her body and held her firmly. Her sigh touched the deepest part of his heart.

"Baxter. Don't let anyone ever tell you you're not good at taking care of people. You're amazing to me." She seemed to settle in his arms, and after several minutes, her breathing deepened, and she fell asleep.

He could have slipped out from beside her and went back to his bed. He could have, but he didn't because he needed her touch as much as she needed his. Sosie brought something to his life. Was it purpose? Passion? He wasn't sure, but it was something that made him want to be everything she needed.

CHAPTER ELEVEN

A distant ringing woke her from a sound sleep, and as she stretched, there was an arm wrapped around her possessively. It was as if it was protecting her from everything she feared about the dark.

She rolled over and burrowed into his warmth. For a man who claimed to fail at taking care of people, Baxter had come to her rescue and become her savior.

With her face pressed against his bare chest, the hairs tickling her nose; she breathed him in. Spicy orange—the same scent that came from decorating the fruit at Christmas with cloves and ribbon.

As he stirred, he pulled her tightly to his chest and pressed his lips to the top of her head. "You awake?"

"Hard to sleep through your alarm," she said.

"I had no trouble. I don't think I've slept that soundly in years." He rolled onto his back. "Hope you don't mind that I stayed." He shifted and tugged her close, so her head lay over his heart, and her body molded to his side. "It was selfish, but you felt good in my arms."

She moved her hand across his stomach, letting her fingertips take in the hills and valleys of muscle created by long hours of hard work. This was one of those times where she wished she could see him if only to confirm her suspicions; Baxter Black was a hottie.

"I slept. I mean, I really slept for the first time this year. I wasn't afraid to be in the abyss because I wasn't alone."

"I'm glad I could help. Sadly, I have to get up and go to work. What are you doing today?"

She rolled onto her back with a huff. It was time to rise and face her reality. "I'm not sure. I thought about what you said—about taking some time to adjust. My life has been a whirlwind since this whole thing began." It sounded like a great idea, but was she thinking with her head or her heart? All she wanted to do was lie in her bed with Baxter, but that wasn't an option either. He had a life and a job, and she wasn't part of his real world.

"I think a break is a good idea. Most people will have a long weekend since the Fourth falls on Monday. There's no reason why you can't put your problems on hold until then."

"What about you? Can't you take some time off? Something tells me you work too much too."

The bed shifted, and when she rolled onto her side to touch him, the heat from his body was still in the sheets, but he was gone. Moving forward, her hand caught the fabric of his sweatpants before he rose from the bed.

"No rest for the weary. I've got another consult this morning, this time with Red."

"Can I come?" It came out without thought. She scurried out of bed and made her way to where the bag of clothes sat on her dresser. "I can be ready in a few minutes. I've become pretty low maintenance." She prayed he would say yes. Spending the day alone with nothing to do was torture. There was only so much television a girl could listen to.

"You want to come to Red's?"

"Sure, why not? It's not like I have a lot to keep me busy." She tucked her hands behind her back and crossed her fingers.

Silence filled the air, and dread filled her heart. Maybe she was too needy. Was asking him to comfort her last night too much?

"I understand if you think I'll get in the way." She picked up her phone and opened the bag. On command, she pulled up the app that told her the color of the clothes. She pointed it at one pair of pants, and it said navy blue. Next came a shirt which was pink.

"Perfect."

He moved to her, "Can I see that? It's awesome."

She handed her phone to him and listened as he pointed it everywhere he could.

"It helps. You should have seen the first time I dressed myself. I looked a hot mess with two different colored shoes on. I have a thing for Vans and put one checkered shoe on and one solid red."

He placed her phone back into her palm. "Get dressed. You owe me pancakes."

She'd forgotten about curtain number three. "Stupid donkey."

"A bet is a bet." He moved toward the door. "By the way, you look damn cute in my boxers and T-shirt."

An excited giggle lifted from her chest. "Maybe you're the one who's blind."

"Fifteen minutes, Sosie, and we're out of here." He pulled the door closed behind him.

Her heart soared with happiness. Minutes later, she heard the shower start. Since she'd had hers last night, she got dressed and walked to the kitchen to make coffee. As soon as he joined her, she rushed off to brush her hair and teeth.

"I could get used to you making me coffee," he called from behind her.

"I made it for me, you're lucky I made enough." She closed the bathroom door and moved to the sink, gripping the porcelain edge, she looked toward the mirror. It was silly, but it seemed the right position to be in to have a chat with herself.

"How lucky are you to be here?" Luck seemed too tame a word when she thought of how things could have turned out. In any other town, they might have tossed her to the curb, but not in Aspen Cove. It was one reason she put her studio here.

The day she googled *studio for rent,* the first hit was The Guild Creative Center. The rent was reasonable, and the landscape surrounding the town was spectacular.

Being an artist who focused on impressionism, it was ideal. She'd painted that meadow a dozen times since she took over the space. In fact, most of the half-finished canvases were probably that scene in different phases of the seasons.

No, luck wasn't the right word, blessed was. Blessed that the town had a man like Doc, who seemed to know what people needed, and a woman like Maisey, who was more like a mother than her own. And Katie, who had the heart of a lion and the generosity of a Samaritan. Then there was Baxter, who pretended he didn't care, or at least he couldn't. No, she had a feeling he was afraid to care, and yet, he did it anyway.

"Are you ready?"

"Coming." She quickly brushed her teeth and her hair and bolted out of the bathroom. It didn't take her much time to get used to the layout of the place, and she skipped down the hallway toward the door.

"I've got your bag." He slung it over her arm and opened the door. The smell of chocolate from the bakery filled the air.

"I could get used to you too." She removed her cane and snapped it open.

"Ladies first."

She made her way down the stairs, taking Baxter's arm when he joined her. "Do you have time for pancakes?"

"You're not getting away from buying me breakfast. I hear you have excellent credit."

She laughed. "It's all I've got."

They walked around the building toward the diner. "Not true. You've got me." He covered her hand on his arm with his. "And you've got a cool app that tells you if your clothes match."

"And a studio full of half-finished worthless art, a mound of debt, and a shitty agent who still wants her canvases."

They entered Maisey's and found an empty booth.

"I've been thinking about that. She said she needed ten Sosie Grant originals, right?"

She touched her silverware and laid it out the way she liked it. Knife to her left and spoon and fork to her right. "Yes, I've had this show on the calendar for close to two years. You'd think I would have tons of paintings ready, but I don't. I have a bunch of stuff that's at various levels of completion. Just proves that you should always expect the unexpected." Maybe that wasn't quite right because she never expected Baxter, but here he was.

"But they're all originals, right?"

"Yes." She tried to figure out where he was going with this. "I do all my own work."

The squeak of Maisey's shoes told of her approach. The scent of honeysuckle announced her arrival.

"Hello, kids, coffee?"

"None for me," Baxter said, "Sosie made a pot before we left the house."

"I'll have coffee." Sosie felt for her cup and moved it toward Maisey. "I didn't get much of the pot I made because he hogged the bathroom, and I had to rush and brush my teeth."

"Sounds like you two are living the marital dream."

She wished she could have seen the look on Baxter's face; she imagined it to be comical, like mouth wide open and bugged-out eyes.

"If marital bliss is a pot of coffee waiting each morning, it can't be that bad," he said.

Her jaw dropped as Maisey poured the coffee. "Juice or milk, then?" Maisey asked.

"Milk and a plate of pancakes."

Sosie held up two fingers. "Make that two plates of pancakes."

Maisey's rubber sole sounds faded into the distance.

"Back to the art."

She frowned. "You said it would be good to get away from what's stressing me. I don't want to talk about art."

"Fair enough."

They sat for a few silent seconds before she spoke. "Tell me about Red's house. Is it a rancher as well?"

"No, a Victorian replica. I have to give the Coopers credit. They can emulate any style and build a kit in no time. The house was put up in two weeks and looks like it's been there forever. It's two stories with gables and gingerbread trim."

"Sounds charming." The description reminded her of the houses in the historical district west of Cherry Creek. "What color is the outside?"

Maisey swung by and dropped off Baxter's milk.

"It's yellow, with white trim and a red door."

"The door seems fitting, given the owner's name. Is the band calling Aspen Cove home?" The population of Aspen Cove was diverse, ranging from bootleggers to millionaires. The people made it interesting.

"They're on the road a lot. Most of them live in Los Angeles but hate the crowds and taxes, so this is where they'll live when they are recording new albums like they are doing now at The Guild Creative Center."

She doctored her coffee with sugar and cream and took a sip. Few things in life offered a trifecta of bitter, sweet, and smooth. Coffee was one of them. Maybe Baxter was another.

"I've never heard them practice, but I've smelled the stuff coming from the culinary center. Samantha's man can cook."

"Dalton is my cousin, and you're right, he can start with a can of beans and a cup of water, and make something gourmet from it."

"I keep forgetting you have a lot of family here."

"It's why I moved here. I was lucky because the town was growing, and Wes needed help. Can you imagine living here a few years ago when it was basically a ghost town?"

She could envision the empty fields and the lake without a soul on it in the summer, untouched like nature intended. "It still would have been beautiful."

A *thud* sounded in front of her, and the smell of buttery pancakes drifted to her nose.

"Enjoy," Maisey said before she dashed off again.

"It must be busy since she seems to rush around." She tuned her ears to the noise.

"The diner is about half-full, but she's the only one on shift. My sister is delivering peacock sculptures to Denver. I heard that Louise's kids have a bug."

"Good for Riley, bad for Louise." She dug into her pancakes and moaned. "So good."

"Killing me with the sounds, Sosie."

Her insides felt warm and fuzzy. Her heart did a cartwheel, and a double flip before it struck the landing. She arrived in Aspen Cove, feeling like her life was over, and today, she thought maybe it had just begun.

As they finished the meal, and she pulled a twenty from her wallet, Doc walked up. She recognized his arrival by his shuffle and aftershave. It was the kind he stocked in the pharmacy, the type that cost less than ten bucks a bottle.

"How are you two faring?" he asked in a gravelly voice.

She knew her face had a wide, silly grin plastered on it. Her cheeks ached from it, but she couldn't make it go away.

"I'm great. Thank you for forcing Baxter to take me on."

"He didn't force me." Baxter piped in. "He convinced me, and I don't regret it for a second."

Her grin turned into a full-blown smile.

"Well, I'm glad to see you two together." He gave her a gentle pat on the back. "You could do far worse than this young man."

"Oh, we're not—"

"Nonsense. I can see it on your face. You're smitten with the lad. As for you, young man, you probably couldn't do much better, so you better lock this one down soon. I hear we've got a lot more competition in town with the band and the new deputy sheriff. Lock it down, I tell ya."

She burst into laughter and reached across the table to feel for Baxter's hand, but found his plate first. When she left her hand in the center of the table, he took it.

"I'm not looking for love, and neither is Baxter, but we're becoming friends." She hoped she hadn't misspoken because she hadn't known him for long, but she shared a lifetime of emotions with him since their first meeting. That made him closer than any friend she'd had in the past.

"Lie to yourself all you want." Doc turned and shuffled away.

"Silly old man," she said.

"Wise old man," Baxter replied.

She took a final bite of her pancakes and considered his statement. Was Baxter feeling the things she was? Was a relationship, despite all the challenges, possible?

CHAPTER TWELVE

At Red's house, Sosie tried to sit in the car, but he coaxed her to come inside and help. She had a good handle on color, and it was fun watching her light up when she talked about how things blended together.

"I hear you're a wizard with color, Sosie," Red said.

Baxter watched her cheeks pink from the compliment.

"Color has always been my passion." Her smile faltered. "I miss it."

"Is there a particular color you miss?" Red asked.

She giggled. "Red, of course."

"It's the best," Red said.

Baxter set his hand at the small of Sosie's back and moved with her to the kitchen. "Red chose painted green, antiqued cabinets."

"What color green?"

He knew she'd want specifics and imagined she could still visualize every color she'd ever seen in her mind.

"I'd call it sage. What about you, Red?"

"I guess. I know nothing about color. All I know is I liked

the aged look, and it seemed to go with my brand-new Victorian."

"There's an oxymoron for you," she said. "What do you plan to do with the counters and floors?"

"I think that's why you and Baxter are here."

"I'd stay neutral." Baxter turned to look at Sosie. "What do you think?"

"I agree. What about something that pulls the dusky tones from the sage like a silver-gray, or if you want something warmer, how about a sandstone or buff-colored counter?"

Baxter pulled a sample brochure from behind the papers on his clipboard, and Red pointed to the fabricated buff-colored stone counter.

They talked about the flooring, which would be a golden oak and picked out tile for the bathrooms.

Sosie's exuberance came forth each time they spoke about color palettes. She lived for color and was now in a colorless world, and he didn't know how she survived.

They left Red's house with a promise to return once the materials arrived. It wouldn't take him long to complete the band members' homes once he started.

Baxter watched her buckle herself into the car and sit patiently until he turned the key.

"Where to now?" she asked.

"I have to work on tearing up the old floors in Merrick's house."

"Oh," her shoulders slumped forward. "I guess I'll go sit in the diner then."

It was obvious she enjoyed spending time with him, and he with her. He questioned the wisdom of bringing a sight-impaired woman to a construction zone. *What could it hurt?*

"Do you want to come with me?"

Her shoulders uncurled, and her chin lifted. "Can I? I promise not to get in the way."

He had a thought but wasn't sure if it was wise. "If you're coming along, you're working."

"I am?"

"Are you feeling frustrated with your situation?"

"Beyond." She shifted, so she halfway faced him.

Was it a habit that made her turn to him like a sunflower to the sun—a learned behavior to face those who spoke to you, or was it something more?

After spending the night in her bed, they seemed like something more. He hadn't made any moves to make it so, but he felt differently about her today than yesterday.

"You can take your frustrations out on the floor."

He drove to Merrick's place and parked in the driveway.

"Do I get to hit stuff?"

"Do you want to hit stuff?"

"Yes, I wish there was one of those places where you can throw plates or bash TVs. I could use a rage room right about now."

"Destroying the canvas wasn't enough?"

"Not by a long shot. I could be a human wrecking ball if you let me."

She unbuckled her seat belt and gripped the door handle.

"How about we start with the kitchen floor?"

"Do I get a sledgehammer?"

"Not sure if that's wise. Let's play it by ear."

He went to the back of his truck, where he kept his tools, and got two pairs of safety glasses, two hard hats, and the weapons of destruction he'd need to remove the tile floor.

With her cane in her hand, she tapped her way onto the sidewalk. Compelled to take care of her, he moved toward her, but coddling her was the wrong move. She needed to be independent, and the foreign desire to care for her needed quelling.

"I'll meet you at the door."

He leaned against the truck and observed her make her way.

His heart shattered watching her cautiously walk to the door. He was one part devastated on her behalf, and the other part in awe of her courage to step forward at all.

He gathered the tools and joined her on the porch. "Today, we'll take out the floors in the kitchen."

"Just tell me what to do."

Once in the house, they moved quickly to the kitchen, where he took the sledgehammer to the floor. Garbed in safety glasses, a hard hat, and one of his flannel shirts to protect her arms, she leaned on the counter and jolted each time the hammer crashed against the tile.

"You want to try it?"

The corners of her mouth turned up and lifted her lips into a smirk. "Really?"

It probably wasn't wise, but it would be therapeutic. "Sure, just give me time to get out of your way." He put the sledge-hammer in her hands and moved back. "Okay, swing it over your head and give it a good whack. When you hit the floor, think of something you despise."

She swung it and laughed when it hit the floor. Repeatedly, she beat the same section of flooring until it was nothing more than chips. She cried out in anger and frustration with every hit.

Tears leaked from her eyes. Winded, she leaned on the handle and sucked in great shuddering breaths.

Losing her balance, she fell to her knees.

The chips had to cut into the denim of her pants and dig into her knees, but her cries didn't change. She let out a consistent wail like the kind when a child is lost and searching for their mother. It was fear-filled and mournful.

He couldn't stand to see her in such pain, so he moved forward and pulled her into his arms. "It's okay. I'm here. I've got you."

She curled onto his lap and held on to him like he was the last tether to her existence.

"I'm so sorry. It's—"

"No need to be sorry. I apologize for putting you in this position. I shouldn't have given you the sledgehammer. Maybe it wasn't such a smart idea."

With her hands wrapped around his waist, she rubbed her face against his shirt. "No, it was good. You don't how much rage I kept locked away. Sure, I'm crying, but it's from the release. I feel lighter than I have in months."

"But you look so sad." He tilted her chin up and thumbed the tears from her cheeks.

"I am sad. There are so many things that I can't do anymore, and I miss those things."

"Like what?"

She took in a shaky breath. "Like run, and dance, and drive a car."

"You can do all those things." He shifted her off his lap and stood. Pulling out his phone, he queued up a song from his playlist. It was a soft ballad by the Eagles. "Let's dance." He took her hand and held it next to his chest while his free hand wrapped around her back to pull her close. While the soles of their shoes kicked up the pieces of tile beneath them, he moved her around the kitchen as Timothy B. Schmit sang about love and loss.

The song came to a close, but they swayed to soundless music that only played in their hearts.

The beauty of the moment ended when her phone rang and told her Theresa was calling. She pulled it from her pocket and stepped away.

"Good morning, Theresa."

He couldn't hear the other side of the conversation, but he could feel the tension in the air.

"You can send it to where I'm staying."

She asked him the address and recited it back to her manager. When she hung up, she appeared more tense than she was when they'd begun.

"What's up?"

He picked up a long-handled scraper and went to work lifting the tile pieces still stuck to the floor.

"She said there was official correspondence she needed to forward."

"That sounds okay. Why the glum look?" What he wanted to ask was why she allowed the elephant to sit in the room. He'd recently banished it, and while it was away for those few seconds, it had grown to twice its size.

"She ruined my dance," Sosie complained.

"Only if you let her. I found out a long time ago that people can only influence your mood if you give them the power to do so."

A slight smile lifted her frown. "You're right." She nodded. "You're so right." She leaned against the counter. "Did you say the band was playing on the Fourth of July at the park?"

"Yep, it should be fun. Would you like to go with me?" It was only a couple of days away. This year, they were doing two free concerts, one on the Fourth· and their annual Fireman's Fundraiser concert in late August. By then, he should have their homes squared away.

"Are you asking me on a date?"

A chuckle bubbled up inside him. "Seems only right since I've already slept in your bed."

"Then, yes. I'll go, but I want to dance again. When I'm with you, I almost feel like myself again."

He wanted her to feel like herself. Losing her eyesight didn't make her less of a woman. In his eyes, she'd have to become more of one given the challenges she would face.

They worked side by side for the next hour. She enjoyed

sliding the scraper along the floor, and he didn't mind doing the cleanup.

While his hands were busy, his mind worked twice as hard. "We danced. Let's work on that bucket list. Losing your sight doesn't mean you have to stop living."

"I think if I ran or drove, that might do me in for good." She swiped at the bead of sweat running from her hairline to her forehead.

"Nonsense." He had an idea, but it would take faith on her part and a big open piece of land. He tugged his phone from his pocket, walked into the other room, and dialed his friend Cade. When he picked up, Baxter said, "I need a big favor."

───────

"YOU'RE INSANE," Sosie said. She gripped the steering wheel so hard her knuckles turned white. He strapped himself into the passenger seat and tugged on the belt to make sure it was secure.

"You wanted to drive. You're driving."

"Where are we?" She turned her head as if she could see where they were.

"Don't worry, there's nothing you can hit. When you're ready, hit the gas. It'll be bumpy because we're in a field, but don't worry. Just drive."

She panted out a few breaths like he'd seen on TV when women were about to give birth, and then she eased her foot off the brake and onto the gas. Slowly she sped up until they were plowing through the field.

Cade had thought he was insane, too, but he was happy to help. His friend had learned recently not to judge. It was a hard-learned lesson that almost cost him his sister and Abby, the love of his life. While he loved the ranch he was building, Cade realized it would be nothing without family.

"Woo-hoo," she yelled as she bounced in the seat. "Can I turn?"

"You better, or we'll hit a fence."

Her beautiful mouth dropped open. "A fence?" She slammed on the brakes, and the seat belt pinched at his shoulder. "I was about to hit a fence?"

"No, not yet, but you can't go forever and not hit something."

She turned the truck forty-five degrees to the left and hit the gas again. "How much space do I have?"

He looked out the window and judged the distance. "A half a mile or so."

"Oh my goodness, this feels so good. I wish this was a convertible. Could you imagine how good the wind would feel in your hair?"

"Roll down the window." He reached up and pressed the button for the sunroof. It slid back, and a breeze kicked up, taking her long strands of blonde hair with it.

He watched the joy on her face, and the light dance in her eyes. When he turned back to face the window, he saw something in the distance coming at them fast.

"Brake! Brake! Hit the brake!"

She shoved her foot down, coming to a screeching halt, but it was a little too late. The truck shuddered when it hit the mass.

"Oh my God, what did I hit?" She threw the truck into park, unbuckled, and exited quickly, running to the front of the vehicle. She dropped to her knees, feeling around. "Baxter, what did I run over? Is it dead?"

He moved beside her and stared at the bale of hay that was no longer in a neat cube and certainly dead. Wyatt must have put it out here to feed the horses that often grazed in the field. "Yep, you killed it."

"Oh, no."

He reached over and removed several pieces of hay from her hair. "Not a breath of life left in it." He collapsed onto the pile and pulled her to him. "It's hay, Sosie. You killed a bale of hay."

She clenched her fingers into her palm and punched him. For someone who couldn't see where she threw her fist, she had perfect aim when she hit the crest of his bicep.

"How could you tease me like that?" She pounded on his chest. It wasn't painful, but playful. "I thought I'd killed a person or an animal." She lifted her nose in the air. "It smells like cows out here. It could have been a cow."

He pulled her down to lay beside him. "There are no cows in this pasture today. I made sure." He caressed her cheek and brushed his thumb against her soft skin. "Did you enjoy the drive?"

Her tongue slipped out to slick her lips. "You don't know how amazing that was. I actually drove with the wind in my hair."

"Sunroofs are a good addition." He leaned in until his lips almost touched hers. "Sosie, I want to kiss you. Are you okay with that?"

"Dancing, driving, and a kiss from a hot guy? Can my day get any better?"

"Probably, but let's not overdo it." He pressed his lips to hers in a soft kiss.

She inched her body closer until they touched from lips to knees. She opened her mouth just a little, but it was enough for him to slip his tongue inside. Velvety sweetness glided across his taste buds, and her moan filled his ears.

One hand moved to her back while the other threaded through her hair. He turned his head slightly for a better angle and deepened the kiss. Tasting, touching, tantalizing each other, they laid in the hay, wrapped up in each other for several minutes until she broke away flushed and breathless. He'd never seen anything so beautiful.

The heat of the sun wasn't nearly as hot as the flames that pulsed inside his body. He wanted more of her—needed so much more, but how could he ask for anything? She wanted someone to give her what she needed, not take what she couldn't give. In that moment, he didn't give a shit. All he knew was that his mouth on hers felt right.

CHAPTER THIRTEEN

Sosie snuck down the staircase while Baxter showered. Today was their first official date, and she wanted to look alluring. At the bottom of the stairs, she turned right and knocked on the bakery door.

Picking up muffins for breakfast yesterday led to a conversation about the Fourth of July community picnic, concert, and her and Baxter's date. Katie offered to help Sosie with her hair and makeup, which she didn't use much of these days since she couldn't be sure it wasn't all over her face.

"Come in," Katie said as soon as she opened the door.

There was a moment of silence where Sosie grew self-conscious. She was wearing the blue sundress she found in the bag of hand-me-downs. She didn't know if it was in good shape or not. For all she knew, it was a mess.

"Is this okay?" She brushed her hands over the soft fabric.

"You look gorgeous." Katie tugged her inside the back room of the bakery. "You don't need to do anything else. You're a beautiful woman, Sosie, and Baxter likes you the way you are."

"Can you believe how this all came about?" A warm,

comforting feeling twisted up her spine and spread through her limbs. "It's all too much to take in—to actually accept."

"Oh," Katie said. "I believe. Don't forget I came here broken and bruised too. I was searching for something. At the time, I didn't think it was Bowie, but I told Sage that when I saw the one, I'd know it, and there he was looking all glum and pissy on that end stool at the Brewhouse. I knew right then he was mine."

"I can't see Baxter, but I feel him," she tapped the area above her heart. "Right here."

"I think you might be luckier to not see him."

Sosie smiled. "Is he ghastly to look at? I don't care because when he kisses me, nothing else matters."

"Baxter, ghastly? No, I don't think he could ever be called that. He's not my type because I like them brooding and grumpy, but Baxter's a good-looking man. What I meant by my statement was you have to fall in love with the essence of a person. Superficial stuff like looks and clothes and cars don't make a difference. When you *look* at a man, you see who he is on the inside. I'd say that's a remarkable gift to be given."

She hadn't considered her blindness a gift, but maybe there were some benefits. "That's not the only thing. I get the best parking spots because even though I don't drive," she giggled, thinking about the day Baxter let her. "I get handicapped parking. I don't freak out when the power shuts off because it's dark in my world all the time." She no longer felt the fear of the dark because Baxter was there. He seemed to sense when it suffocated her, and he pulled her closer to let her know she wasn't alone. "I can read all night long and not wake anyone with a light."

"You learned braille?"

She smiled, feeling proud. "I did. Though, I'm slow at it. It's not second nature to me, and I have to translate it in my brain, so it's a process, but I can read."

"Do you have any books?"

She shook her head. "No, not with me. I was reading Harry Potter, but it's at my apartment. When I drove up here, I wasn't expecting to stay."

"You're bilingual. That's so cool. I'm glad you're looking at the bright side of things. When I was living in the hospital, I had to find the shiny gold nuggets in my life of coal. Some days it was a visit from an old friend, and at other times, it was the chocolate pudding."

Sosie had heard all the stories about the townsfolk. In a small town, all you had to do was keep an ear open and someone was always telling a story. If you paid attention, you could learn a lot.

"How is your heart now?"

She heard Katie thump her chest. "It's full."

"I should hurry. Baxter will wonder what happened to me."

"Right. Can't keep the man waiting on his woman."

That thought thrilled her. "I'm not his woman. He's just a good guy who got saddled with me. Thankfully, he doesn't seem to mind."

"When I get through with you, he won't let you out of his sight."

Katie styled her hair and helped her apply mascara. It was funny how she hadn't worn it unless someone could help her put it on. She pinked her cheeks with a sweep of blush and slicked her lips with something she called a stain.

Sosie turned in a circle, making the hem of the dress float out and come down to skim her thighs. "Is the dress good? I don't have a big spaghetti stain on the front or anything, do I?"

"No, it's perfect. In truth, it never looked as good on me."

Sosie's eyes opened wide. "This was yours?"

"Yes, it would seem that you and I are the same size."

"Lucky me," Sosie said.

"No, lucky me. I was happy to clean out some stuff. I've got another bag for you at home. I'll bring it by tomorrow." She set her hands on Sosie's shoulders. "Let nothing stand in the way of your happiness." She turned her around, so she faced the door. "Now, go get your man."

Sosie's heart beat hard enough to bruise her chest. Would Baxter be pleased, or would he take one look at her and run? Was this the direction he thought they were going—a direction that would take them somewhere different. If she could just see him, she'd know what he was thinking, but she couldn't, so she went with her gut feelings. Trust wasn't something she used to give easily, but now she had to have blind faith, or she wouldn't be able to navigate her life.

She climbed the stairs and opened the door. The smell of his body wash and cologne floated in the air.

Heavy footfalls approached her, then silenced. "Baxter, is that you?"

The wood flooring squeaked, and hands touched her arms and moved up to her bare shoulders. "God, you're stunning."

She laid her hand flat against his chest and moved it until she touched his strong jawline. Her fingertips slid across his smooth, just shaved face to his lips. Full lips that knew how to pull moans straight from her empty lungs. She brushed over his cheekbones and up into his hair.

"You're not so bad yourself."

"The other day you said I was a hottie; how do you know?"

"I feel it in my heart. I'm not talking about your looks, though I'm told you are a nice-looking man."

"Oh yeah, by whom?"

"Don't get your hopes up that there's another fan other than Mercy. Katie is married and has her own sexy man."

"I don't know if I like you thinking any other men are sexy."

"You're the only sexy man I'm interested in now."

"Now?" His lips brushed against hers. "Planning on dumping me soon for a better model."

She lifted on her tiptoes and touched her lips to his. "I'm quite satisfied with the model I have."

"Oh, sweetheart. I haven't even begun to satisfy you."

A shiver of need raced to her core, where it heated and throbbed. "I like the sound of that."

His kiss was a promise of things to come. Things she could only imagine.

"We've got to go, or we'll miss the barbecue, and I need a store of energy for what we're doing tonight."

Giddy excitement filled her. She hoped all this teasing wasn't simply that. She'd spent the last few nights in bed with Baxter. The only thing separating them was his sweatpants and a sense of honor.

THEY FILLED up on burgers and chips and found a spot of lawn where Baxter laid out a quilt to save their space for the concert and fireworks. He took her from booth to booth, where vendors set up to sell their wares.

"I'll take that one," Baxter told the person behind the counter. Moments later, she felt a braided piece of leather being tied to her wrist. In the center was an etched metal in the shape of an oval. "What does it say?"

He rubbed his thumb over it. "Fearless. I think it's fitting."

"I'm afraid of everything."

"Not true. You are a warrior."

She stood a little taller with his praise.

She pulled her sunglasses from her bag and put them on.

"Sunglasses?"

She nodded. "Sure, I can still get cataracts, and sometimes, I can see shadows and flashes of light. Like today, I can tell it's sunny, not only because I'm breaking a sweat, but somehow, the brightness leaks through the dark."

"Interesting. What else do you see?"

She held his hand. "I swear, occasionally, I get a glimpse of stuff for a nanosecond like my retinas are talking to my brain. It doesn't happen often, but it happens sometimes."

"Like the blue couch?"

"Yes, like the couch. I can't tell you anything else that's in the apartment, but I knew that sofa was blue."

They moved forward, Baxter guiding her through the crowd. "Do you believe in fate?"

She stopped and lifted her eyes toward him. "Do you mean like meeting the perfect person at the right time?"

"Sure, but more than that."

"There's more than epic love?" The smell of waffle cones floated around them. "Is Sam's Scoops here? If so, I'd say that was fate because I'm dying for an ice-cream cone."

They moved to the back of the line. "Seriously, I've been thinking about your life. All you've done is paint. You've said it yourself, your whole world was nothing but paints and canvases. What if going blind was the universe's way of telling you to open your life to other possibilities?"

They moved forward a little at a time.

"I would have rather received an invitation to try something different. This was baptism by fire."

He entwined his fingers with hers. "Seriously, would you have accepted a chance to change your life?"

"No, because I didn't think I needed a change. I still eked out a living. I could take a couple of jobs a year, and I had what I needed."

"What's the Albright job?"

The mention of it made her stomach ache. "It's a massive canvas of their ancestral home. I'm to show all four seasons in the same painting. Imagine starting out in the gardens in spring and walking past the castle-like structure in winter. It takes so long to move across the property that you experience all four seasons on the journey."

"That sounds amazing, but now what?"

After a heavy sigh, she said, "I'll have to find a way to pay them back or figure out how to paint blind."

"Sosie, the painting you worked on was amazing until you smeared it and tore the canvas. Even then, I think it's remarkable. That's why I kept it."

"It's trash, toss it."

"It's not, and I'm keeping it. You said I could. Are you taking it back?"

They made it to the counter, and she breathed in the sweetness. "I'll have a single scoop of Chocolate Dingleberry."

"How did you know that was one of today's flavors?"

She had no idea. Was it another case of her seeing something she couldn't? "I think I heard someone say the name. Anything that's chocolate is okay in my book."

He ordered the same, and they made their way around the field and back to the blanket on the grass. The cool air raised gooseflesh on her skin, which meant the sun had already set.

Baxter offered her a jacket he'd brought along "just in case". He was the most thoughtful man she'd met.

"Tell me, the other day at Gray's, you jotted perfectly scaled walls and flooring on the paper. How did you do that?"

"I pressed into the paper with the pencil and that left lines. I guess it was like braille. I felt my way across the page." She knew what he thought. "It's not possible. The canvas gives, so I would lose the impression in seconds, and if you think I can follow the paint lines, then you're wrong too. The paint stays wet too long, and I'd smear it trying to find the end of my last line."

"You already tried that. That's why the canvas I have is smudged."

"Yep."

"We'll figure it out. When do you have to have the Albright painting done?"

"I have until the beginning of August to get Theresa her pictures, and until March to get the thirty grand. It's a huge undertaking, but as soon as they found out I lost my sight, they worried. I'm holding them to the contract, even if I can't deliver. That will at least give me time to come up with a solution."

"Don't you have any paintings to sell. What about the stuff you did as a child?"

She found it endearing he'd done his homework. "My mom has a few, but I'm not asking her for them."

"Not even to help you?"

She shook her head. "Nope."

The strum of a guitar silenced all the surrounding voices. She sat between Baxter's legs, leaning against his chest.

She closed her eyes and took in the beat of the drums, the rhythm of the bass, the thrum of the guitar, and Samantha's sweet voice. The words were hauntingly fitting for her life.

Never give up.
Never give in.
It's not over until it's over.
Life is a dark place.
Look for the light.
It could be in a voice, in a touch, or a scent on the wind.
Don't give up.
Don't give in.
It's not over until it's over.

When the final song finished, the first of the fireworks soared into the sky and exploded with a boom. She kept her eyes closed and let her memory fill her mind with a picture.

"Tell me what you see," she said to Baxter.

His lips were close to her ear. "I see a breathtaking woman

who makes me feel more vibrant than the colors in those fireworks."

His whisper against her ear did all kinds of things to her body. His words did the same to her heart. When her world was turned upside down, she resigned herself to a life of loneliness, but Baxter Black changed her mind about that.

"Thank you. I feel so many things when I'm with you."

"Do you want to feel more, Sosie? Are you ready for more?"

"So much more," she said on the exhale of a breath. She leaned back and listened to the explosions overhead. Each one got her closer to the end. Or was it the beginning?

The air crackled with excitement as the last boom sounded. They stood, and she waited off to the side while Baxter folded the blanket.

Consumed by the herd of people, she got jostled and pushed in every direction. "Baxter," she called as the momentum of the crowd took her away. She didn't have the time to pull out her cane. It took everything to stay on her feet.

In the distance, she heard her name. "Sosie," he screamed. "Sosie, where are you?"

She could hear the fear in his voice.

She lifted on her tiptoes, hoping to make herself taller so he could see her. "Baxter, I'm here," she screamed. Someone ran into her from behind, knocking her to the ground. She was certain she'd get trampled to death when strong arms wrapped around and swept her up. "I've got you." He buried his face in the crook of her neck and kept up the mantra, "I've got you. I've got you." He said it repeatedly. Was he trying to convince her or himself that she was safe?

"You can't run off like that. I turned my back, and you disappeared."

She laughed because if she thought about her fear, she would fall to pieces. "I got swept away in the crowd. How many people are here?"

"Thousands." He held her tighter and moved through the crowd with her in his arms.

"Do you have the blanket?"

"Nope, it doesn't matter. All that matters is you're okay. God, Sosie, you scared the hell out of me."

"You? I wasn't sure where I'd be once the momentum stopped."

"I told you, I suck at taking care of people."

She wanted to believe he was joking, but she heard the disappointment in his voice.

Reaching up, she gripped his chin and forced it down, so he had to look at her. "I don't need you to take care of me. All I need is for you to care for me."

By the silence around them, she knew most people had moved past. He dropped her legs, and she slipped down his body.

"I care about you."

She tossed her purse over her shoulder and threaded her fingers through his. "Then take me home and show me."

CHAPTER FOURTEEN

Performance anxiety had never been a thing for him until this moment. He asked her if she was ready for more, but was he? Having a girlfriend was scary enough, but a blind girlfriend put a new twist on things.

Though she claimed to be capable of caring for herself, he'd seen firsthand that she couldn't, and neither could he.

"Your hand is shaking," she hugged his arm.

"I lost you in the crowd. That was my fault. I'm so sorry."

"Not your fault at all. It's not like I got swept out to sea. I got jostled in the throng of people and lost my direction. I would have been okay. You could have left me, and I would have used my phone to get back."

She gripped his arm like he might get away.

"I would never leave you Sosie. Seems to me like too many have done that in the past."

His step faltered, but he knew it was the truth that tripped him up.

"It feels like you're leaving me already. I get it. I understand being with me is a challenge. Don't think if I had my eyesight back, it would be different. I've always been a challenge."

"It's not that. I told you already; I'm a bad bet. I'm oblivious when it comes to the needs of others, and I have a hundred-percent failure rate making sure people are cared for."

She let go of his arm and stopped. "You're so full of shit. You've done nothing but nurture and care for me this whole time. You got saddled with a babysitting job, but you rose to the occasion, and for that I thank you."

She pulled her cane from her bag and unfolded it and moved forward, leaving him behind.

"Where are you going?"

"Back to your apartment. I don't want your help Baxter, and I don't want you if you're not willing to trust in what we are building together." She pointed from her to the direction he stood. "You and I, we were special."

"You are special."

She laughed, but not in that funny, humorous way. "Yep, I'm special all right." She moved down the street with him following. "A special kind of annoying and frustrating and needy, but I don't need you. I wanted you in a way that I haven't wanted anyone else because you got me, or I thought you did."

His heart was near bursting with everything from want to fear. He got her, and that scared the hell out of him.

"Sosie, you are ..." what did he say when she was everything he wanted, but the thought of letting her down terrified him. "More than I deserve." He moved toward her and when she stopped, he brushed away the hair that had fallen across her eyes. Those eyes that somehow saw into the deepest part of his soul. "You and I are special. Chance brought us together, but I love you by choice."

She leaned forward until her head rested on his sternum. "The only thing I have left to offer is my heart and my trust, what will you do with it?"

He repositioned himself with one hand on her back and bent over to sweep her into his arms. Once he had her secured, he moved quickly toward the back of the bakery, and the staircase that would take them home. *Home ...* It had a nice ring to it.

"What are you doing? Put me down."

"I'm taking you to bed. My bed where no tears have been shed and no fear of the dark has been felt."

"Oh," she giggled. "Carry on then."

He took care not to hit her head on the wall as he took two steps at a time. When they got to the top and realized the door was locked, he groaned.

"Reach into my pocket and grab my keys."

She reached down to fumble for his pocket and skimmed over his hardness. "Oh, wow. That's impressive."

"You're killing me, Sosie."

She lifted her hand in the air with the key swinging from her index finger. "Got it."

After a few misses, she unlocked the door. As they moved down the hallway with her in his arms, she kicked off her shoes. They hit the wooden floor with a thud.

"Don't forget those are there, I don't want you to break your pretty little neck in the morning tripping over them." He set her on the edge of the bed. "God, Sosie, you literally take my breath away."

She reached out and tugged on his belt loops. Losing his balance, he fell onto the bed next to her. They lined up on their sides facing one another.

"Are you sure about this?" she asked. "I don't want this to happen because you feel sorry for me, or because you feel guilty. I don't want to be your pity fu—"

He covered her mouth with his, delving in to taste her sweetness. He nipped and nibbled at her bottom lip until it plumped.

His hand skimmed over the hem of the dress, lifting the soft fabric up her thighs—smooth velvety skin with goosebumps dotting the surface.

He wanted to touch every part of her, fully explore the canvas of her body. His insides shook with need, but he took his time. At the back of her dress, he tugged the zipper tooth by tooth until half the fabric fell to the bed. The other half, he teased off her shoulder and worked down her body until only her sweet lace bra and underwear remained.

Looking at her lying there made him want to bite his knuckles, pound his chest, and scream she was his. He had an almost feral need to claim her.

Her delicate fingers pulled at the hem of his T-shirt, working it up until she couldn't move it anymore. He rose to a seated position to pull it over his head.

"I wish I could see you unwrap yourself. It feels kind of like Christmas."

"Sosie, it's Christmas in July, and you're everything I've been asking Santa for since I could remember."

Her hands slid over his chest, and he wondered if she felt the same tingle he did in her fingertips, an electrical current that danced at his nerve endings.

"Tell me about you, what color is your skin? Are you fair like your sister or tawny from days in the sun?"

"I'm darker than my sister in every way. Dark hair, dark eyes, and tan skin. If we didn't come out of the same womb minutes apart, my father would have thought Riley wasn't his. I favor him, but Riley looks exactly like the picture we have of our mother."

"I can see you in my mind. I've put together what I know and what I feel, and you're perfect."

Her hand moved to the button of his jeans where he covered it with his own. "This will change everything."

She pressed her lips to his chest. "You've already changed everything. I'm more than I ever thought I could be because of you."

He shook his head. "No, you're just more." His lips met hers for a languorous kiss.

She tugged and pulled at the button until it sprang free. The zipper went next. Seconds later, he shimmied out of his boxers and jeans.

He lay naked next to her lacy underwear and closed his eyes. He wanted to experience everything the way she did—through touch.

With the slip of his fingers under the elastic of her panties, he tugged them down inch by inch.

"My eyes are closed," he said.

"Why," she said in a throaty whisper.

"I want to experience our first time the way you do. Raw and unfiltered with touch, taste, scent, and sound as our only way to explore." He unhooked her bra and tossed it aside. Keeping his eyes closed, he worked his hands over her body.

To feel her like this was thrilling. It struck him as funny how seeing dimmed his other senses. The synapses in his brain fired each time he heard her moan, or felt her breath hitch. He didn't need his eyes to please her.

A brush against her nipple pulled a mewling, needy sound from her throat. The ghost of his touch along her hip sent her body thrusting toward him, grinding against his length. He touched her everywhere, tasted her in all the places he dreamed of, and kissed her senseless.

Her breath hitched when his tongue stroked her. She combed her fingers through his hair when he kissed her.

This was it. He gloved up and hovered over her, pressing gently inside her. Behind his closed lids, he relived the fireworks of the night. Blasts of red, white, and green flashed as he sank himself deep inside her.

Their bodies moved together effortlessly. They shared a rhythm that, somehow, they both knew.

He kept the pace steady but shifted his position several

times until her raspy breath and sexy moans told him she was close.

"So good," he said.

"Oh, yes." She wrapped her legs around his hips, pulling him deeper into bliss.

He never knew it could be this good. Take away his sight, and everything else compensated. "You feel incredible," he said as he moved inside her in a way that seemed to set her on fire. And when his name burst from her lips, and her body shuddered beneath his, he let himself surge free in that moment.

Sinking next to her, spent but satisfied, he opened his eyes to find her cheeks pink, her hairline damp with sweat, and a smile on her face.

"Oh my God, is that the way it's supposed to be?" She rolled toward him and rested her head against his chest.

With his hands wrapped around her, he rolled onto his back, taking her with him.

"It was damn amazing. I swear, I saw fireworks."

"I see them all the time."

He frowned and went still. Did she mean that all sex was firework worthy? "Every time you have sex?"

She shifted until she was comfortable with her naked body draped over him like a blanket.

"No, I meant that behind my eyelids, I see flashes of color. Red, white, green, and occasionally I swear I see blue and gold. Tonight, I saw a full spectrum of color. Every shade of the rainbow and everything in between."

He relaxed beneath her. "Sosie, thank you for being with me —for trusting me with your body and your heart."

She laughed. "I know when you said you loved me earlier, you didn't mean true love, but I like the way you make my heart feel. It's as if you've stitched my hurts up and made me whole again."

"You were always whole. Meeting you has made me think

about how much our vision hinders us. We look at people and judge them by their appearance, or their expressions, and never take the time to see a person for who they are. When I say you're beautiful, it's not just your looks. Although, you're hot by any standard." He ran his hands over her bare back. "When I look at you, I see a woman whose strength lies in her heart. You give everything you have to those around you. Tonight, you gave me your body and your heart, and I promise to keep it safe. When I said, I loved you earlier, I meant it. There is so much to love about you, Sosie, from your courage to your sweetness to the little mole above your right breast."

"You said you didn't look." She moved on top of him, getting a reaction he wasn't sure she was ready for.

"Oh, I looked, but that was before I closed my eyes and felt you. You seeped into my pores like honey—sticky and sweet and so good for me."

His length bobbed against her, and she giggled. "Round two?"

He spent the next hour loving her more than he knew possible. When it was over, he pulled her back to his front and wrapped his body around her like armor. Sosie was here, and she was his, and he'd do everything in his power to be the man she needed.

CHAPTER FIFTEEN

"What's going in here?" She brushed her foot across the flooring of the kitchen.

"I'll pull up the tile and make it all hardwood, but would it be easier for you if the flooring changed? That way you'd know where you were in the house."

Baxter moved toward her and pressed his body into hers. His lips brushed over her neck until he found the lobe of her ear. "What do you want?"

She gripped his hips and pulled him closer. "Do you even have to ask?" Since that first night of lovemaking five days ago, they'd been inseparable. She worked by his side during the day on his other projects and at his house at night.

He wanted to finish it so they could move in together. It was all happening so fast. Her heart told her to go full steam ahead, but her mind told her to slow it down. It was two against one because her body was in sync with her heart.

"I love that you're considering me in your choices, but this is your house."

He bit her lobe, hard enough to sting, but not cause

lingering pain. "What are we doing here, Sosie? We're together, aren't we?"

Her head nodded before the word yes came to her brain. "Yes, we're together."

"Then what do you want to have in your house."

"I love the look of hardwood. What about if you saw several lines at the transition? I'd be able to feel the ridges with my cane and my feet."

"Transitional ridges it is. Now let's get on to the good stuff. We're nearly done and have to pick out the finishing touches. What color granite do you want?"

She laughed. "I don't care. I can't see it, so what does it matter?"

He placed his hands on her cheeks and kissed her lips before taking a step back. "You might not *see* it, but you'll know what's here, and you will picture it in your head. If it's not what you like, then it's not good. Haven't you ever imagined a house of your own?"

"I used to have a loft in Denver. That was before ..." She moved her hands through the air.

"Before you lost your sight?"

"No, I gave it up prior to that. My brother needed treatment none of us could afford, and I downsized so I could help."

She could almost see him shaking his head. "I don't get it. Why aren't they here helping you? Where's your dad?"

"Last I heard he was living in Montego Bay with his third wife."

"And your mom?"

"Told you already, she's in Tuscany."

"Right, living off your paintings."

"It's not like that. I haven't told her I'm blind."

"What? Why not?"

"Because she couldn't handle it."

"When does your brother get out of rehab?"

"I'd say any day now. He'll call when he's released."

He kissed her forehead. "I'm here, and I'm not leaving. If you want to get rid of me, you'll have to leave me first."

"I've made love to you. Leaving you after that is unlikely. Living without you is like living without air. Can't be done."

"Glad to hear that. I feel the same way." He leaned in and kissed her. "Now, back to the stone, what do you want?"

She loved him for his consideration. "I'd love a stone with lots of neutral colors. I once saw something called butterfly beige. It's black and white with patches of earth mixed in. I'd love to see that with antiqued cream cabinets and a soft-beige paint with warm undertones."

"Consider it done."

He was on the phone within seconds, spouting off measurements and colors, and when he hung up, he threw his hands in the air, or so she thought. It was one of those times where she was certain she'd seen the action, but after a blink of her eyes, she knew she couldn't have. She rubbed her eyes and blinked several times.

"You okay?"

She cocked her head side to side, trying to get the kink out of her neck. "Did you just fist the air above your head?"

"Yeah, why?"

She shook her head. *Did I see that?* She closed her eyes and tried to figure it out. If she saw it, would she have taken in everything else around her? "Are you wearing a blue shirt?" That's what her brain said.

"No, it's green." He lifted her chin. "Are you okay?"

"Yeah, I think so. Just tired."

"Let me put my Sosie Grant original on the mantel, and we'll go."

He moved away, and something slid across a surface in the distance.

"You didn't put that awful piece over the fireplace, did you?"

"I did. It's beautiful. You called it Rage, but it's not that at all. It's the day you let your fears die, and you were born again. You accepted what the universe had given you and made it work. It might have been the day I fell in love with you."

He'd said those words to her countless times, and each time was like the first. They never ceased to amaze her or fill her with warmth.

"I love you too, Baxter Black. You add color to my life." Her stomach grumbled.

"Maybe it's time I added nutrients to your body."

"Is that what we're calling it today?"

"Let's go to Maisey's, and then to the Brewhouse for a beer."

"Are you asking me on another date?"

He wrapped his arm around her shoulder and walked her out of the house—their house.

"I guess I am."

It was a short drive from the house to the diner. When they walked inside, his sister greeted them both with a hug.

"Where have you two been hiding?"

Sosie could feel her cheeks heat. Her damn pale skin always gave her away.

"We've been busy." Baxter walked her over to the booth on the wall, where she sat the first day they met. He'd dubbed it their booth, and as long as it was unoccupied, they always sat there.

"Ben has cleaned up the kitchen and won't dirty it, so if you don't want him to burn your food in protest, I'd order the special. Tonight is chicken and waffles."

She never understood the combination but liked them separately. "Sounds good to me, but can I have them on separate plates? I don't want syrup on my chicken."

"You got it," The light thud of her shoes faded as she walked away.

"What about me?" Baxter called after her.

"You get what I bring you," she yelled back.

"Siblings, they're a pain in the ass, and yet, I love her to pieces."

Sosie smiled, thinking about her brother. "I can't wait until you meet Gage."

"I look forward to it. Maybe he'd like to move to Aspen Cove? When he's not in treatment, where does he live?"

She shrugged. "When he had a job, he lived in Phoenix, but as things got worse, he couldn't keep up with rent. He couch-surfed until he ran out of friends. Drunks have a way of burning bridges."

"I'm sure he could use the apartment until he gets his feet on the ground. What job skills does he have."

"He's charming," she said. "All the women like him."

"Yeah, not sure there's a gigolo position open in town. What did he do for a living before his life turned to shit?"

"He's dabbled in a lot of things. I'm not sure he ever really found his passion."

"There are a ton of people here who could help with that."

She reached across the table and took his hand. "Isn't saving one Grant enough for a lifetime."

"No, sweetheart, I know you'll never be happy if he's not okay, and I want to make you happy."

The bell above the door rang, and she instinctively turned her head to face it. "Who just came in?"

The bench beneath Baxter squeaked. "It's Jake, Natalie, and Will."

The sound of a herd of cattle shuffled across the floor. Or at least that was what six feet sounded like to her. Lately, all of her senses were on overload.

"Baxter, good to see you."

She glanced in the voice's direction.

Baxter squeezed her hand. "Sosie, this is Jake Powers, and

next to him is Natalie. She used to wait tables here at the diner, but now she runs the bookstore."

"Oh," Sosie gushed. "I totally forgot about the bookstore. I'll have to stop by."

A hand settled on her shoulder. "You come by anytime," a sweet voice said.

"Are you blind?" a boy's voice chimed in.

"Will," Natalie scolded.

"What? It's a reasonable question. Why would she want to come to the bookstore when she can't read?"

Sosie laughed. Months ago, that would have destroyed her, but now that she'd settled into her new life, it didn't faze her.

"I can read. Only I do it with my fingers." She raised her hand and moved her fingers. "I was halfway through the first Harry Potter book when I came here and forgot it at home."

"I'll be right back," Jake said.

"You like Harry Potter?" Will asked.

She felt the bench dip beside her, and a body nudged her over.

"I do. Wouldn't you love to be a wizard?"

"Sure," came the young boy's voice from beside her. "Only I wouldn't want to live in a closet under the stairs. I lived in my sister's cardboard box for a while, and I imagine it's a lot like that."

Sosie raised her brows. "A cardboard box?"

"It was a tiny house, not a box," Natalie corrected.

"Don't let her fool you. It was a box, but I moved here and saved her."

Baxter's hand still sat below hers from across the table. "There seems to be a lot of saving going on around here," she said.

The bell above the door rang again, and a breeze followed the person to their table. "This just came in." A thunk sounded on the table. "Sorry it took a little longer, but it was harder to get than I thought," Jake said.

Baxter's hand pulled out from under hers. "Thanks so much."

"Oh my gosh, is that Har—"

"Let's go, young man," Jake said. "I'm starving."

"But that's Har—"

"Now, Will. Let's leave them be," Natalie said.

They were gone a few seconds when the smell of waffles passed before her. "Waffle to your left and chicken to your right," Riley said when she set the plates down.

"Is that Will's?" The air moved next to Sosie, and there was a thud as something hit the table.

"No," Baxter said. "That's Sosie's."

She was thoroughly confused. "What's mine?"

"I'll be back," Riley said and dashed away, leaving behind her scent of tropical fruit.

Baxter slid something across the table until he touched her fingertips. "I thought you might miss reading. I ordered you the first Harry Potter book in braille so you could finish it."

She gripped the edges of the book and pulled it to her chest. "You got me a book?"

He laughed. "Not just any book. It's Harry Potter."

"When did you order this?"

"The day Katie told me you left it behind."

She set the book down and slid from the booth to join him on his side. "And you claim to not be nurturing." She cupped his cheeks and pulled him in for a chaste kiss. Later, she'd show him how grateful she really was.

"I tell ya, there's something in this mountain air that hits the heart," Riley said. "I look at you two and see how you both bloom in each other's presence." She tapped Sosie's shoulder. "Don't break his heart, or I'll try to burn down your studio again." She let out a laugh that filled the restaurant.

"Go for it. By the end of the month, it's not mine, anyway. I've got a new career. Turns out, I'm great at laying tile."

"I wouldn't say great,"—Baxter teased,—"but you're a work in progress," He slid over, so she had more room next to him. The scrape of her plate sounded against the Formica when he moved it in front of her. "Waffle to your right and chicken to your left."

She reached to her left to touch him. "I'd never call you a chicken," she joked. "You were brave enough to take me on."

CHAPTER SIXTEEN

"You've got mail." Baxter walked into the kitchen and kissed Sosie on the cheek while she stirred the pasta sauce. It still made him nervous each time she cooked, but he was getting used to it after a week of home-cooked meals. Besides, she was a good cook, and her pasta was his favorite.

"Who's it from?"

He glanced at the corner of the envelope. "I think it's your agent. Theresa Branton, right? This is from the Branton Agency."

"Don't open it. It will most likely ruin our dinner."

"What if it's a check?"

She laughed. "I haven't received a check in a long time. You have to sell something to get a check." She pulled a strand of spaghetti from the pot and held it on a fork. "Come taste this and tell me if it's ready."

He slurped the noodle into his mouth and chewed. "It's perfect, just like you." He took two plates from the cupboard and set the table.

It hadn't taken much time to adjust to each other. They seemed to move like a well-oiled engine.

She drained the pasta while he pulled the garlic bread from the oven. She dished up the meal, and he got the parmesan cheese. They sat down to eat.

"You can't ignore it."

"Yes, I can. Whatever is in there won't be pleasant."

"Rip it off like a Band-Aid."

She twirled the spaghetti onto her fork. "Fine, read it to me."

He ran his knife under the envelope flap to open it and pulled out a single sheet of paper. He read through the legalese of it.

"You're right, it's not pleasant."

"What? What does it say?"

"She's suing you for breach of contract unless you produce ten pieces of original art by next week."

She slammed her fists on the table, jarring their dinner plates and sending a piece of garlic bread into the air. "I told you it wasn't good."

"Come on, Sosie, what can she sue you for? Even you said you have nothing." He couldn't imagine what Theresa had to gain from the threat.

"It's not what she'll take from me that matters; it's what she'll take from my mother. The house in Tuscany is in my name. If she sues me, my mother will lose her home."

He took a breath to calm his frustration. When was someone going to look after Sosie's best interests? As soon as he considered it, he realized that was his job now.

"Your mother is an adult, she'll be fine."

She pushed her plate away. "No, she won't be fine. She's a shell of a woman since my father left, and the house is all she's got."

"Not true, she's got Gage and you."

She palmed her eyes and rubbed. "What good is a blind artist and an alcoholic son going to do her?"

He might have a solution to her problem. "Hear me out. The other day we were talking about your art, right? You mentioned that Theresa needed ten Sosie Grant originals."

"I don't have ten canvases to give her."

"But you do. You have at least that many in the studio."

She shook her head. "None of which are finished."

"What if you finished them?"

She let out a growl that could send a guard dog into hiding. "I know you're a smart man, but you're not thinking. I tried to finish them, and it was a disaster."

"You're wrong. The painting in my living room at the new house is amazing. It's not the old Sosie Grant art, it's different, and that might be okay. This is new, and it's raw and authentic and fabulous. What if you took the collection—"

"Geez, Baxter, it's not a collection. It's a bunch of shit that I should toss away."

"Just give me a chance to explain," he pleaded. He knew if he could get her to listen to reason, then she might have a solution. "You're blind."

"Brilliant observation, now what?"

Frustration pricked at his skin. "You don't have to be mean; I was only trying to help."

Her shoulders rolled forward, and resignation settled in her downcast eyes. "I'm sorry. What's your idea?"

He pushed her plate toward her. "You eat while I talk."

She picked up her fork and began twisting spaghetti again. "Wow me with your plan."

He smiled. "I will. We both know that you're afraid of the dark, but your fans don't. I was thinking about the canvases at the studio. They are all in some stage of completion. What if we lined them up from the least finished to the most finished? On the unpainted area ..." This is what he'd need to sell her. "Make it black and call the collection *Out of the Darkness*."

"But I'm still in the dark."

"Are you?" He leaned back in the chair. "Seems to me you've found some light in your life. Whether that's me or the town or reading or laying tile, you've walked through the dark and have found a way to the other side."

She gnawed on her lower lip, and when it popped from between her teeth, she scowled. "That's not what people expect from me. It could ruin my reputation as an artist, and that's all I have."

He closed his eyes and prayed for strength. "That's all you have? Really, Sosie?" He slid his chair out and stood. "Who am I to you? What does what we've been building together mean to you?"

"You're everything," she whispered.

"No, I'm not, and I don't expect to be everything, but I want to be something. Something more than a soft place to land for a few weeks. Make up your mind. On one breath, you say you need to save your mother's house, and on the other, you're worried about your reputation. You're a blind has-been artist that needs to live in the present and not the past. I thought I was part of that present." Once the words were out, he wanted to snatch them back but couldn't.

"You don't know what you're talking about. I'm not a has-been!" she yelled. "My art still sells."

"What art, Sosie? There will never be another painting if you don't risk something. You do what you want, but I'm done trying to help." He turned and walked away.

"Where are you going?"

"Out." He marched out the door and slammed it behind him. Once he hit the cool night air, he walked down a few stores and entered Bishop's Brewhouse from the back door.

Loud music and awful voices assaulted him. "Karaoke night. Great." He found an empty seat at the bar next to Doc, who sipped his nightly mug of beer. In front of him was a napkin with tic-tac-toe squares drawn on it.

"Did you win or lose?"

"Tonight, I'm buying my own beer."

Cannon set a frosty mug of Budweiser in front of Baxter and left to fill empty pitchers.

"Must be a losing kind of day."

Doc turned and lifted a bushy white brow. "Trouble in paradise?"

"This mess with Sosie is all your fault, Doc."

"Now listen here, son, I asked you to give her a bed, but I didn't mean yours."

"You're right. I'm just in over my head, and I don't know what to do. I can't make her see reason."

"She's blind son, it will take her a while to see anything. I imagine what she can't see with her eyes, she sees with her heart. Sosie seems like a nice young lady, and it will take her time to accept her new way of life."

"I get that, but she was doing great, and then something happened today, and it all turned to shit."

Doc took another drink and licked the foam from his mustache. "What happened?"

He wasn't sure if he should tell Sosie's story, but he needed help, and in a roundabout way, it was his story too.

"Her agent will sue her for breach of contract if she doesn't send ten completed canvases to Denver within the week."

Doc rubbed at the scruffy white hair on his chin. "Seems harsh to me, but business is business, and so it's within her right to sue. If Sosie can't produce what she promised, then she is in breach of contract."

"But she's blind. Shouldn't that account for something?"

"It should, but it won't. If she didn't have a clause in the contract to void the deal, should she become unable to create the work, then she needs to produce the art or pay to settle the claim."

He told Doc about his idea for a new Sosie Grant collection. Doc sipped his beer and listened. "I'd say you've come up with a good plan. Something is better than nothing."

"You'd think, but she's not on board." He tipped back his mug and drank deeply, then set the glass on the wooden bar with a bang and pulled out cash to pay for it. "I should go check on her."

"Now that's where you're wrong. Give her some time to think about what she's up against. Imagine being her. She probably feels like one of those milk jugs at the carnival. You know the ones that everyone lobs balls at. She's been dodging balls for months. Might not be bad if one or two hit her. Could knock some sense into the girl."

Doc was right, Sosie needed to attack this problem on her own. If everyone kept saving her, then she'd never be able to save herself.

"My biggest fear is letting her down. Don't you think abandoning her when she needs me the most is the same as failing to take care of her?" He slid his empty mug forward and nodded to Cannon to fill it up.

Doc shook his head and sighed. "Seems to me you're making her problem your problem." He turned to look over his shoulder. "When you and I sat at that table over yonder, you told me you couldn't let her stay with you because you weren't good at taking care of people. Son," Doc patted him on the back. "Part of caring for someone is knowing when to let them make their own choices. Seems to me like you gave her a good idea. Whether she runs with it or ignores it, is her decision and not your problem."

Cannon set the new beer in front of him. "You look like hell. Since I don't see Sosie sitting next to you, I imagine your hell has blonde hair and blue eyes."

"And she's as stubborn as an angry goat," Baxter added.

"Welcome to the women of Aspen Cove. You can't live with them, and you can't live without them."

Doc tossed a five on the table. "My work here is finished. Lovey is making pot roast tonight, and we're watching Golden Girls."

As soon as Doc was out of earshot, Cannon said, "Just shoot me if my greatest thrill becomes pot roast and Betty White."

"How is Sage?" Envy filled the lower half of Baxter's heart. Most of his friends were married with children, or in Cannon's case, with a child on the way. "Is she feeling well?"

"Baby is growing. She's six months along, and every night when I lay my hand on her stomach, I can hardly believe my kid is simmering inside of her."

"You know what it is?"

He shook his head. "Nope, it's not like we'd send it back either way. There are few surprises in life these days, but the sex of our baby will be one."

Life surprised Baxter all the time. Especially since Sosie arrived. "I'm happy for you, man. I really am."

"What about you? I'm assuming you had a disagreement with Sosie, and that's why you're here alone."

He thought about what Doc said. "I'm giving her time to figure some stuff out."

"That's man talk for it's not safe to go home."

Baxter chuckled. "I see you have some experience in these matters."

Cannon rubbed the side of his head. "My Sage has perfect aim, whether it's a shoe, a glass, or one of those pinecone candles we once had on the table. *Had* being the important word. But regardless, making up is the best part of the fight. It's how the little Bishop got in her belly."

Baxter thought about Sosie and what it would be like to

have a child with her. There would be challenges for sure, but nothing was insurmountable. *I'd fail both of them.* His mind went back to his dead father and his scarred sister.

"I'm not sure I'm cut out to be a father. What if the apple doesn't fall far from the tree?"

"If that was the case, Bowie and I should have stayed single and kept our pecker in our pants. Don't forget that our father was the town drunk. I always thought I'd failed him, when in reality, he failed himself, and in doing so, failed us."

That hit Baxter in his already bruised heart. He'd been blaming himself all these years for his failures, and not once did he see it as his father's, but the fact of the matter is, how was a kid supposed to raise his parent?

"He got his shit straight, though, right?"

"He did, and that's because Sage and Katie thought he was worth saving and made him believe it too. Your aunt helped a lot in his recovery. She filled his hollow heart with love. I'm telling you, man, a good woman can make all the difference in your life."

Cannon rushed off to fill pitchers and take payments while Baxter ruminated on all the mentoring he'd received that night. Once he finished his second beer, he paid his bill and headed home.

He climbed the stairs, wondering what he would find. Would she be up? Asleep? In his bed? In hers?

"Sosie," he called from the front door. "I'm back, and I'm sorry."

Only silence and the hum of the refrigerator compressor greeted him. He went to the kitchen and found it spotless. Garlic scenting the air was the only clue that they had served dinner that night. He moved down the hallway and peeked into her room, thinking she would have climbed into her bed if she was still angry, but it was empty. He passed by the bathroom and expected to find her in his bed, but when he flipped the switch on, only an empty bed and a note greeted him.

Baxter,

You were right.

Sosie

Right about what?

CHAPTER SEVENTEEN

The tip-tap of her cane on the sidewalk kept her focused on the task at hand. She needed to get the canvases painted. One way or another, she would deliver something, but perspective was always a challenge. She didn't live like anyone else and didn't think like anyone else. Her brain was wired differently, or maybe that was her excuse.

A cool breeze blew around her, crickets in the distance sang their night song. Night. It was night, which meant it was dark. She tuned into the sounds around her. There was a laugh nearby, and the lap of water rushed the shore of the lake, the rustling of something in the bushes to her left.

"What I can't see can't hurt me." It was a stupid thing to say. Everything she couldn't see could hurt her and did.

Baxter promised he'd never leave her, and he walked out. She sat crying into her plate of spaghetti until she remembered crying never helped. All it did was stuff up her nose and make her eyes itch.

His idea wasn't awful. It would get her out of the jam she was in. The contract said she had to deliver ten original works of art. It didn't say impressionist art. She could toss paint against the canvas and call it such. She'd seen many an artist get hundreds of thousands of dollars for abstract work.

"Turn left in fifty feet," her app said. She did her best to gauge the distance, but she had to trust the accessibility map would get her to her destination. "Turn left in ten feet." She moved forward, and her phone vibrated in her hand. "Turn left now. Your destination is one hundred feet on your right."

That was to the front door. She needed to enter at the back —the door that led directly to her studio. Going in the front would pose all kinds of challenges, like finding the alarm panel to disarm it so she could travel freely down the hallway. She didn't have an alarm on her back door because she often left it open while she painted, and no one could set the alarm to the building, so they bypassed it.

When she rounded the rear of the building, she tucked her cane into her bag and used her fingers to count the doors as she passed them. She was the ninth and last door in the building. She'd chosen this unit because of its stunning views of Mt Meeker and the valley below it.

At her door, she put in her key and unlocked it. The sweet smell of linseed oil washed over her. To some, it was unpleasant, but to her, it was home.

She left the lights off and went to work gathering the canvases leaning against the walls. One by one, she touched them to feel where the paint ended and the canvas began. Why she hadn't depended on her other senses, she didn't know, but she figured it was because the event had completely blinded her emotionally. She'd tucked herself into the dark, awful place where she wallowed in sorrow, selfishness, and fear.

Only nine of the pieces had enough work to call them art, and she stacked them next to her easel. Thankfully, Baxter was taking care of her. He'd set her paints out in order of the color wheel and set the black and the white next to the colored tubes.

Tying her hair back into a ponytail, she went to work. Her

phone rang several times, but she ignored it. She was in the zone. The paint slid across the canvas as if the brush were moving on its own. She was too talented an artist to simply blot on black. She needed depth and color to get her point across. She was the black moving toward the light, and as she moved the paint toward the pre-painted section, she let hope shine onto the canvas. In her mind, it looked a lot like a dark sky opening up and a ray of light guiding her on her path back to herself. Not her old self, but her new self.

By the fifth time her phone rang, she knew she couldn't ignore it any longer. The only person who called her was Baxter, and he deserved more than her silence.

"Hey," she said as she mixed what she hoped was a stormy blue-gray.

"Sosie, where are you? I'm worried sick about you. I've been calling, and I went by the studio, but the light was off. Where are you?"

It warmed her heart that he cared so much. Theresa had been right when she said she should have had more people supporting her. The problem was, she didn't know how to let others in. It wasn't something she was used to. She did the supporting, whether it was empathy for her drunkard of a brother, or sympathy for her depressed mother. She was the rock in her family, and there was no one to help her.

How funny that a stranger had to show her she had value beyond her art, and that her work could exist, but differently.

"Sosie, are you there?"

She shook all thoughts from her mind. "I'm here. I'm at the studio. I don't need lights."

"I'll be right there."

"No, I have to do this by myself. Thank you for the brilliant idea. You were right."

"But I wasn't, you're not a has-been, at least not to me. You're everything."

He'd used her words. "Thank you. I needed to hear that, but right now, I have to be everything for me. I know that sounds selfish, but there can't be us if I can't close the chapter on my old life. I need to do that in a way that honors my art. I'm using your idea to rework these canvases. I can see them in my mind, and they are amazing."

"When will you come home?"

"Not until I'm finished."

She expected him to argue, but he didn't. Baxter Black understood her. He might have been the only one who had taken the time to figure her out.

"Call me when you're ready. I'll pick you up. And Sosie ... I love you."

"I love you too. Thank you for being exactly what I needed."

She went back to work and didn't stop until she finished the ninth canvas, and her fingers cramped so badly she feared they looked as knobby and gnarly as the twisted branches beyond her window.

She gathered her things and extended her cane. Her phone told her it was five in the morning. Had she painted all night long? She turned to look over her shoulder as she walked out the door. The canvases were there even though she couldn't see them, and she imagined they might be her greatest work yet.

She considered calling Baxter because she was dead on her feet, but the brisk morning air invigorated her. She told her phone to map her path, and she moved down the street toward home.

The weight of the world lifted from her chest. She would make her deadline, and with any luck, she'd earn enough money to pay off the Albrights. She didn't have ten canvases, but she had nine original works of art, and that was more than she could hope for.

As she moved down Main Street, a calm she'd never felt before settled over her. Birds singing, and the sound of an oscillating sprinkler leaked into her awareness. Bacon and syrup scents filled the surrounding air.

She trudged up the stairs and walked down the hallway. Sleeping in her bed was probably what she should have done, but she missed Baxter, so she kicked off her shoes and climbed into bed next to him. His arms wrapped around her and pulled her close. Even in sleep, he loved and protected her.

She closed her eyes and let the exhaustion pull her under.

———

HIS ABSENCE WOKE HER. She felt the coolness on his side of the bed and knew he'd left for work hours ago. Today he planned to finish Gray's house, and then move on to his. He'd laid down the hardwood floors and used a circular saw to put grooves in between rooms for her. Today the counters were coming—counters she'd picked out because he wanted her to be happy where she lived.

She rolled onto her back and covered her eyes. Her first hint that something was wrong, or maybe right, was a sharp pain that nearly split her head when she opened her eyes. The bright light of the room was almost blinding.

She closed her eyes, thinking what she saw was a ghost of a memory. Something from her past that was playing tricks on her mind.

She moved her hands in front of her face and slowly opened her eyes again. Shadows of pink floated in her vision. Nothing was clear, but there were color and texture mixed in with the cottony blur.

"Oh my God!" she screamed. "I can see."

She tripped over her shoes while jumping out of bed. She brought them to her face. "Vans, I've been wearing white tennis shoes all along, and I never used the app because I thought they were black." She tugged them on and raced to the bathroom to look at herself in the mirror.

"You're a mess, girl." She leaned in until she could focus on a single square inch of her skin. As she waited, more came into focus. "My face." Her palms cupped her cheeks, and she pinched them the way an Italian grandmother did her grand-children. Pink rose to her skin. She rubbed at the dark circles below her eyes, but the smudge didn't come off because that was what happened when she didn't get enough sleep.

She threaded her fingers through her hair. How she missed seeing strands of blonde and beige, gold and brown. "You need a haircut."

Curiosity didn't kill the cat, but it mesmerized her. For the next hour, she moved around the apartment, seeing it for the first time.

"Blue couch." It was the exact blue she thought it was and wondered if she'd seen it. She touched the books on the shelf, looked out the window that oversaw Main Street, and watched as people moved from shop to shop.

She should have called Baxter right away, but she'd lived in the dark for over six months, and she wanted to bask in the light by herself for a few minutes. Wouldn't it be funny if she pranked him the way he had Red and Gray? Only she'd be pretending she was blind when she could see.

She picked up her phone and saw the cracked screen, broken from so many drops and falls. She dialed Baxter's number and waited for him to answer.

"Hey, Sosie, did you get some sleep?"

"Slept like the dead. Where are you?"

"I'm at the house. The counters just came. Should I pick you up?"

She held back a giggle. "No, I'll walk. Should I bring you lunch?"

"It's almost dinner. How about we eat at Maisey's?"

"Sounds perfect. I can't wait to see what kind of pie she has tonight."

"It's always the same."

"I know, but I want to see for myself. I'll be at the house within the hour." She knew he wouldn't pick up on what she meant. She always used the word see even though she couldn't before.

She hung up and called her agent.

"I see you got my letter. I thought you'd ignore it." There was no friendly hello or how are you. It was strictly business. She almost blurted out that she could see, but Theresa didn't deserve to be the first one to know. That privilege was for those she loved.

"I tried, but Baxter convinced me to take a peek."

"And?"

"I'm calling to tell you your art is ready. I only have nine canvases."

"I need ten."

"Fine, you'll have ten. I have no way to transport them, so if you want them, come and get them." She swallowed the lump in her throat. She was telling Theresa to pick up art that even she hadn't seen.

"Is the paint still wet?"

"I used thickened linseed oil, so it will be surface dry."

"I'll be there tomorrow."

Sosie's heart fell to the floor of her stomach. "Tomorrow?"

"The show is next week, Sosie. It's a good thing you called because I was signing a different artist."

Being replaced should have made her feel something like anger or jealousy. She felt nothing. "Okay, tomorrow then."

"All ten, that's two less than you promised, and they better be good. We can probably punch up the price given that you're blind. That's almost as good as being a child prodigy. Glad to see you're back. Plan to ride home with me, and we'll discuss the future."

As soon as the call was over, she sank onto the couch. Her future? Wasn't it here with Baxter? If she thought living in the dark was scary, making her way back to her old life felt like climbing a waterfall. She wasn't the same person she was six months ago, she was broke but rich in so many ways.

All she wanted right now was Baxter and one of his hugs.

CHAPTER EIGHTEEN

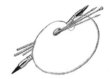

He had installed the sink in the kitchen just as the door opened, and Sosie walked in. She looked lit up like a Christmas tree. Painting all night must have filled her soul with goodness. Never had he seen her look so pretty.

"Hey, you." He wiped his hands on his jeans and moved toward her. Her eyes got bigger as he neared to brush a kiss across her lips.

She smiled and raised her hands to his face, running the pads of her thumbs across his cheekbones—across his lips. With spread fingers, she combed through his hair like she hadn't felt it a hundred times already.

"Dark chocolate."

"Or mud," he said, knowing she was asking about the color of his hair. She did that a lot. Asking for specific colors helped her picture things in her mind.

"No, it's like sipping chocolate, smooth and rich and deep brown."

"You can call it what you want as long as you kiss me."

She did, she pulled him to her and kissed the breath straight from his lungs. When she stepped back, she turned in a circle as if taking in her surroundings. It was odd for her, but he'd learned to expect the unexpected with Sosie. She was one of a kind and unpredictable.

She moved to her painting like a moth to a flame. On tiptoes, she stretched her fingers to touch the checkered shoelace he'd used to close the gaping hole in the canvas.

"Interesting. I like it." She took a step back and narrowed her eyes like a critic. "I've never used multimedia in my paintings, but I find it fitting. You did the same for me that you did for this painting. You took in a girl with a broken heart and stitched up the deep cut with your love."

Sosie was always intuitive about her work, but this time, she seemed to see what was in front of her.

"Sosie, what's going on?"

She spun around to face him. "I can see!"

"You what!?"

"It's not perfect, there's a halo around everything like my world is surrounded by frayed cotton, but I see everything."

His heart skipped a beat. "Like really see? As in you see me?"

She nodded. "I see you in your tattered jeans and cotton T-shirt. The shock in your big brown eyes is heartwarming and scary at the same time." She threw her arms out and spun in a circle. "I see your beautiful house." She rushed to the kitchen and touched the granite counter. "This is exactly the way I pictured it."

He stood glued to the hardwood floor. She could see, and that would change everything. Would she stay with him? He couldn't imagine she'd choose him. Her life differed from his. She was art shows and galleries, exhibitions and consignments. She had a home in Tuscany and a place in Denver. The only thing she came to Aspen Cove for was her studio.

He knew it should thrill him, and he was happy for her but devastated at the loss of the Sosie he knew. She would get buried behind the Sosie of old—the artist who needed paint and linseed oil more than love.

"That's great, Sosie." He swallowed the lump that nearly choked him. "It's really great." He moved to her and hugged her tightly. "Shall we go out to a nice place for dinner and celebrate?"

She shook her head. "Maisey's sounded like a great idea, but I realize I have so much to do. I have to go to the studio and get the canvases ready because Theresa is coming tomorrow to pick everything up."

"Are you going too?" He sucked in a breath and held it, waiting for the one word that would crush his soul.

"Yes."

He took a step back from the emotional punch to his gut.

"Right." He moved to the sink and started on the plumbing.

"I'm coming back, Baxter. I promise."

He smiled, even though it took every bit of effort to keep it there. "Sure, your studio is here."

She rushed to him and threw her arms around him. "No, I'm coming back for you."

He set the wrench on the counter. "I appreciate that you think you'll come back for me, but, Sosie, you have a life outside of Aspen Cove. It's a life I can't give you here."

"Then come with me to live in Denver." Her skin glowed with excitement. "We can get a cute little fixer-upper in the historic district."

He shook his head. "I'm flattered you offered, but my home is here. I've got a good life in Aspen Cove, and my family is here."

"Are you breaking up with me?"

Was I? "No, Sosie, I'm just pointing out that I'll be here, and you'll be there. Things will be more difficult, but maybe they can work out. I mean ... you seem to have a pocketful of miracles."

KELLY COLLINS

"Oh my God, you are breaking up with me."

"I'm just being realistic. Wasn't it you who said if you can't be an artist, then who are you?"

She crossed her arms over her chest. "That was before I met you."

He pulled her into his arms and hugged her like it might be the last time because deep in his heart, he knew it was.

"You are a strong, sexy woman who showed me that love is possible, and caring for someone isn't as risky as it seemed." He forced a chuckle. "Hell, I might even be a little good at it. I mean, you survived me."

She buried her nose in his chest and breathed deeply before she stepped back. "I'm going to the studio for a bit. Let's meet back at the apartment for a celebratory glass of wine."

Losing Sosie wasn't something he wanted to celebrate, but the return of her eyesight was. How could he be unhappy about that? "Have you called your doctor?"

Her headed bobbed. "I called him on my way over here. He thinks it was stress that caused the swelling to remain, and as I relaxed into my acceptance, my body healed, and the pressure on the optic nerve subsided. I have an appointment with him the day after tomorrow."

With little more to say, he nodded. "Do you want a ride?"

She looked over her shoulder at the painting on the mantel. "I could use a ride and that painting if you don't mind loaning it to me. I need ten canvases, and I only have nine."

The painting would be all he had left of her when she went back to her life, but it wasn't truly his, he'd kind of hijacked it that first day in the studio.

"It's yours, Sosie, take it with you."

"I'll give it back." He dug into his pocket for his keys. "Let's get you and the painting over to the studio."

He moved around the house he thought he'd share with her. She was everywhere, from the color of the walls to the transition lines in the flooring. She was in the speckles on the granite to the blue sea-glass tile he had yet to install in the bathroom. Sosie might not live with him, but she'd always surround him.

He turned off the lights, grabbed the canvas, and walked out the door.

HE SAT at the bar with a beer clutched between his palms. The icy frost that melted onto the bar mimicked the puddle of tears he wished he could cry. Life was a bitch. It gave you a taste of something great, and then it pulled it back.

The stool next to him squeaked against the flooring when the person pulled it out and took a seat.

Baxter didn't need to look at who it was; Doc was the only man he knew who still wore Old Spice.

"Looking glum there, my son." Cannon dropped off a beer, a napkin, and a pen.

Doc drew the nine boxes for his daily tic-tac-toe game and set the pen on the bar.

Cannon picked it up and made an X in the upper left-hand corner, and Doc took the middle box of the right-hand column.

"Isn't it better to claim the center first?" Baxter asked.

Doc shook his head. "There's more than one strategy to get what you want."

Cannon placed an X at the bottom left-hand column and Doc blocked the win with an O in the center. In two more moves, Cannon had won.

"You lost Doc, what kind of strategy was that?"

The older man turned toward him. "By the look on your face, I'd say you need to talk. By losing, Cannon gets paid by you because my counseling services aren't free."

Cannon nodded toward Doc. "And that's why he's the

smartest man in town." He turned and disappeared into the stockroom.

Baxter looked around the mostly empty bar. The only customers were two of the Lockhart brothers, and Goldie and Tilden, who all sat in the corner table, whispering like they were planning world domination.

"Do you want to tell me about it, or do I have to beat it out of you?"

Baxter pulled the mug to his lips and drank deeply, letting out a sigh when he placed the mug on the bar.

"Sosie's sight came back today."

Doc hit the table and let out a whoop that startled everyone. "That's amazing. Why are you here instead of with her?"

He let his head hang. "She's got a gallery thing and needs to get her canvases ready."

Doc sipped his beer. "Oh, I see. She's moving back to her old life."

Baxter turned to face Doc. "Why would she stay here?"

"You're here, that's why."

He chuckled. "What can I offer her that Denver can't."

A bear-like growl came from Doc. "Love," Doc reached out and popped him on the side of the head. "You love the girl."

"I do."

"Does she know?"

"She does."

"And she's still leaving?"

Baxter finished his beer and held his mug up to catch Cannon's attention to get another.

"I can't expect her to give up her life for me. She thought her life was over, and she settled for me. I'm sure she thought I was the best she could do."

Doc's hand smacked him on the ear again.

"Ouch. Why are you doing that?"

"To knock some sense into you, boy. Love is rare and valuable. Never underestimate the value of your love. That girl probably hasn't ever been appreciated for who she was. You didn't care that she was some fancy painter, or that she was broken."

"She wasn't broken. She was perfect." Baxter's hackles rose at the notion that Sosie wasn't perfect.

"That's what I'm talking about. You saw her soul. How many people do you think have had that opportunity?"

They hadn't talked about other relationships, so he didn't know. When Doc's hand raised again, Baxter covered his ears.

"She's coming back, Baxter. Just make sure she knows she's welcome. How much trust did it take to move in with you? She didn't know you. She had to have faith that I was doing right by her and that you would as well. She let you into her heart and her bed. I'd say that's the most vulnerable she's ever been, and she depended on you to care for her. Now it's time to trust her to come back."

Doc finished his beer and moved his mug to the edge of the bar. "My work is done here. Go home and make love to your woman. Send her on her way with something to miss." He slid off the barstool. "Don't forget to pay for my beer and tip Cannon well. He's got a baby on the way, and diapers aren't cheap."

Baxter settled his tab and went home to make sure the apartment was lit with candles, the tub filled with bubbles, and his heart bursting with love. He'd give Sosie a sendoff she'd never forget.

CHAPTER NINETEEN

It was days ago, but her body still ached in all the right places, and her heart ached. If she closed her eyes, she could see the candles twinkling around the room, the flowers on the table, and a look on Baxter's face that said he didn't think she'd ever come back.

"Open your eyes, Sosie," Dr. Patterson said. "I want to see what your optical nerve looks like." He'd dilated her eyes and taken pictures with some fancy equipment.

"Mm-hmm, yep. I see." He spoke in short affirmatives. "Not perfect, but in the right direction. I'm going to put you on another course of steroids to see if we can't get the remaining swelling to go down, but I think you're out of the woods." He moved the equipment to the side and sat back. "Tell me what happened in the last four to six weeks that changed everything because I didn't think you'd get a reversal."

"I fell in love."

Dr. Patterson's brows lifted, leaving a crease in his forehead. "Love cures just about everything."

"He helped me to see my life in a different way."

"Interesting."

She pulled an invitation to the gallery from her pocket. "I've got a show on Saturday if you want to attend. I finished all the paintings when I was blind."

"Fascinating." He tucked the invite into the pocket of his jacket. "No driving, yet. I think you can get by with over-the-counter readers, but I want to see you next month."

She left feeling both happy and sad. Happy that her eyes were healing, and sad that Baxter wasn't there to share in her joy.

She arrived at the gallery to supervise the hanging of her art. The order was important.

Last would be Baxter's painting. Theresa said it was the best of the lot because there was so much emotion. Rage was the perfect name for the moment it was painted and destroyed, but all she saw now was love. She named the picture *Love is Blind* to honor the journey she'd taken since painting that piece. She moved to the starting canvas, which was mostly dark and scary. Black paint swirled in a vortex until it touched the light in the corner. It was just a peek of the meadow, a sliver of hope too small to recognize. As she moved through the pieces, she noticed things she hadn't seen before. Tiny messages hidden in the movement. Words like truth and passion buried beneath the layers, but not too deep to be silenced. Those were the things that Baxter taught her. He gave her the courage to accept, and the strength to press on. He filled her heart with love and her body with passion. He saw her soul in a way that no other man could have. She saw him for the person who lived in his heart and mind, not the hot construction guy who made her body quiver at night. God, she missed those nights.

They'd chatted several times a day, but it wasn't the same as holding him and feeling his heartbeat beneath her ear while they snuggled together. His voice was distant, and she was sure the miles between them had nothing to do with it. It was the distance she'd put between them when she left.

As if her thoughts summoned him, a text came in.

Got your invitation.

She waited as the three dots danced across her screen, stopped, and danced again, only to stop.

Will you come?

More dots moved, and it seemed like an eternity for him to write his answer.

She held her breath and waited and waited and waited.

Yes, I'll be there. "Yes," she yelled. **I love you.**

No dots danced across her screen in response. She'd lost him, at least for that moment, but what about forever?

"I have to say, this show will be amazing," Theresa said, reaching over her to straighten the frame. "I've already got offers on the *Love is Blind* piece."

"I told you, it's not for sale."

"Don't be silly, of course, it is."

Sosie shook her head. "No, it's not. It's not mine to sell."

As soon as she had pieces of art, Theresa became her best friend again.

"That wasn't our agreement."

Sosie moved to the next piece. "So, sue me."

Theresa stuttered. "You know that I only sent that to give you a kick in the pants. It appeared to do the trick. Call it tough love."

Sosie searched for the word in the background and found *power*. "Love isn't tough, Theresa. It's compassionate and understanding, and it's forgiving. And because I have a certain love for you, I will forgive you for being such an awful person and leaving me in a diner. You abandoned me, and that might have been the most loving thing you did because I realized that your love of art and money and fame drove me all these years.

You're the one who made me feel like I was nothing without my art, but you're wrong." She moved to the next canvas, which showed ripples of color moving out from complete darkness to blend in with the meadow, which took up half the canvas.

"Oh, Sosie, you're something. You're a beautiful young woman, but art is who you are."

Funny how Theresa's tune changed when everything went back to status quo.

As she progressed down the row, the pictures grew lighter and happier and showed the love floating from the tip of her paintbrush.

"No," she looked at Theresa. "Art is not who I am, it's what I do, or ... what I did." She turned and walked out of the gallery.

"What are you talking about?" Theresa called after her. "I've already committed you for several pieces and a show in Paris next year."

Sosie stopped and turned around. "Sorry, I've packed up and moved out. I've got tile to lay, paint to choose, and a man to love."

"You are not going back to that little, nothing town."

"Aspen Cove? It's not nothing. It's everything. He's everything."

"You're making a mistake. The world needs what you offer. You owe it to your fans to continue."

"I owe myself a life, and that's my new focus."

She laughed all the way home. Baxter Black didn't think she was coming back. What would he think when he couldn't get rid of her?

She nearly skipped to her apartment, where the movers were finishing packing up her stuff.

She tipped them generously, knowing she wouldn't be destitute once the new paintings sold.

"I'll let you know in the next few days where to deliver my

stuff," She told the man in charge and followed them into the hallway before she closed the door on her old life.

Being blind had been scary because she had no choice. Now she was uprooting her life and trusting that love would guide the way because she believed the right man could make a difference—had made a difference-- to her world.

On her way to the Brown Palace Hotel, she dialed her mother, who picked up after the first ring.

"Sosie, sweetheart, how are you?"

"I'm good, Mom." She hadn't told her mother anything that had gone on over the last six months, including her loss of vision. After her nervous breakdown, April Grant didn't have the fortitude to deal with stress. She was better off sitting on her veranda, painting, and thinking all was right in the world.

"What's new with your art?"

That had usually been the topic of conversation because they both had a love for anything artistic. "It's been slow, but I'll be okay."

"I've got some of your earlier pieces we can auction if you need the money, honey."

Sosie laughed. "No, mom, I'm okay. I have a show tomorrow that should get me out of the pickle I was in."

"Speaking of pickles," her mother giggled. "Is your brother in trouble again? I haven't heard from him."

"He's enjoying a spa month." That was what they always called rehab. While it wasn't hot stone massages and pink champagne, she always sent him to the best places.

"I don't know what to do for him, but I'm grateful you're always there."

"That's the thing, mom, you can't do anything for him. He has to want to do it for himself. I have faith that he's turning a corner, and he'll figure it out." She wasn't sure that was true, but she didn't have the resources to save him from himself any longer.

"And you? Are you figuring it out?"

"I am. I've got this new art that is my magnum opus. I painted them blind." She didn't go into detail. Eventually, word would leak out and make it to Tuscany that Sosie Grant had temporarily lost her sight, and she'd get a motherly call chastising her for not reaching out for help.

"Why would you do that? You're an incredible impressionist, Sosie. While I'm sure you could paint a masterpiece in your sleep, never chase fame or fads."

"It's not that at all. I'll send you a picture of one." It was the least she could do since she was the one who cultivated her love of art, who gave up everything, including her own career, so Sosie could become the painter she is. "Mom," her heart raced just thinking about the pieces. "They're raw and real and painted from my soul. I thought I should go out with something people will talk about for years to come."

"Go out? What do you mean?"

"I'm moving on. I fell in love, and I'm following my heart."

"I'm so happy for you, honey."

Love had never been kind to her mother. In fact, love hadn't been kind to any of them. It wasn't a conversation mother and daughter had, given her father's betrayal and her family's suffering, but Sosie knew now that everything was possible, including love.

"What about you, Mom? Will you open your heart to love?"

There were long seconds of silence. "I have. I'm with Dante." It came out in a quick confession.

"Dante, the plumber?"

She thought there had been an unusual number of leaks and fixes needed on a fully renovated house.

"He's so much more than that. He's everything. Now tell me about your man."

Sosie spent the entire forty-minute walk talking about Baxter. By the time she climbed the stairs and entered the hotel lobby, they were ready to say goodbye. Her mother's final words were, "Always choose love."

She was choosing love, but would the man she loved choose her?

CHAPTER TWENTY

He hoped Doc was right about the sport coat and slacks without a tie. He'd tucked a blue one in his pocket in case he needed it.

On the sidewalk, he looked through the windows of the gallery, hoping to get a peek of Sosie before he went inside. It was better to get the heart pumping dizziness out of the way, so he didn't make a complete fool of himself.

The packed gallery held hundreds of people ambling about, drinking champagne, and eating tiny pieces of toast with who knew what on top.

He presented his invitation to the person at the door and asked if she knew where Sosie Grant was.

Obviously, the woman was a one-time hire because she looked at him with confusion.

"There are five collections on display tonight, is she one of the artists?"

"No, she is *the* artist." He half considered taking her position at the door. He would know at least twenty percent of the work. Then again, he hadn't seen the finished product before she packed up the canvases and left.

He should have insisted on seeing them. Maybe she left him because she didn't think he supported her work. He was just another person telling her to move on. He shook his head. That wasn't true, he'd put her in front of a canvas and asked her to paint. Her work had hung proudly in a place of prominence in his house because he loved it, and he loved her.

He grabbed a glass of champagne from the waiter's tray as he passed and downed the first glass, chasing after the man to get a second.

He moved past paintings that were colorful but lacked the passion that Sosie's did. She bled her soul straight into the paint. Her heart was in every stroke of the brush.

He moved from piece to piece, looking for her and her work. He turned the corner and froze. In front of him was his piece or the piece that used to belong to him. He didn't harbor any resentment that she took it back. It was an original and could bring her a lot of money. What made him unhappy was having nothing to remember her by.

"It's magnificent, isn't it?" a man to his right said. He slid his glasses from the tip of his nose to the bridge. "Too bad it's already spoken for. I would have paid anything for this piece." He moved his hands back and forth in front of the canvas without touching it. "You can see the emotion in it. There's everything there from rage to love. It's aptly named *Love is Blind,* don't you think?"

Baxter wasn't an expert in art, but he felt he'd become an expert in Sosie in the short time she was there.

"There was passion there, all right. Sosie Grant has a way of pulling out every emotion a person can feel." Right now, he felt somewhat lost. This was her life. Art was her world, and he knew nothing about it. The man next to him could probably talk to her about it all day long, and they'd never run out of things to say.

He didn't like thinking of Sosie with any other man than

him. Hundreds of thoughts had gone through his mind the last few days. Thoughts about what he had and what he wanted. She'd asked him to come to Denver, and he flat-out refused her. That was the equivalent of telling her she had no value beyond what she brought him in Aspen Cove.

He moved backward through the art until the dark overtook the light, and his emotions matched the tone.

He stood staring at the first painting, where only a corner of it showed color. This was what his life felt like now. Even the blue and green sea-glass tiles he put in the bathroom seemed dim when she wasn't there.

Realization hit him, and he knew that being with Sosie was far more important than living in Aspen Cove and owning his house. He told her his family was there, but it wasn't if she was gone.

His skin tingled a second before her voice reached his ear. "You came."

He spun around to face her. "I told you I would."

Looking at her standing before him took his breath away. Dressed in royal blue, her eyes shone like gemstones. She'd trimmed her hair and styled it, so it fell in soft waves over her shoulders. Her makeup highlighted her eyes, and her lips glistened pink under the overhead lights. He took her in from the top of her head to the pointed tip of her heels.

"You're beautiful."

She gripped his lapels and tugged. "Not so bad yourself."

"I missed you." He wanted to kiss her so badly his stomach hurt, but this was a high society affair, and he was certain tugging the star artist into the nearest closet wouldn't go over well.

"I missed you too. I'm sorry I had to leave." She looked around at the art hanging before her. "This had to be done. I had commitments."

"I understand. This is your life." He swallowed hard. "We

really need to talk about things." He wanted to blurt out the words, *I'll go wherever you are*, but the timing was all wrong. Tonight was about her. About her success, and her path back from darkness into light.

She leaned in, and just before her lips touched his cheek, her agent walked over. "Myron Straight would like to talk to you."

"Oh," Sosie smiled. She took his hand and tugged him forward. "Come with me."

"Just you, Sosie." Theresa gripped his arm and yanked him back, and for a second, he felt like they were playing a childhood game of monkey in the middle.

He released Sosie's hand. "Go ahead, I'll be here."

"I remember you," Theresa said. "You sat at the table next to us in that diner."

He nodded. "Yes, that was me."

Theresa pointed to where Sosie stood next to a man who looked like he jumped off the cover of GQ Magazine.

"That's her future," Theresa said. "Her new stuff is taking the art world by storm, and he owns galleries all over the world. He has what she needs to make her great again."

"She's already great, and her newest work is amazing." He felt a sense of pride knowing he had something to do with the direction she went in.

"Where can you take her?"

He snapped his head from Sosie's to Theresa's. "What do you mean?"

"That man right there," Theresa nodded toward the guy she called Myron. "He has the power to give her everything she wants—everything she needs. He's an eagle that she can soar with; you're a weight that will drag her down."

He narrowed his eyes. "Is there a reason you're telling me this?"

With beady eyes and a cunning smile, she said, "I'm looking

after her best interests, and while she might think she's in love with you, you need to think about it. You took her in and gave her a place when she was vulnerable. That's not love, it's gratitude."

"You don't know what you're talking about."

"But I do. I've basically raised that girl. I'm like her mother."

"Some mother. You abandoned her when she needed you the most." He knew a lot about being left behind.

"That wasn't abandonment; that was tough love."

"That was bullshit. You cut and run when she was useless to you."

"But it sure benefited you for a while."

"Now that she's back and her new art is a hit, you're here."

"As are you. Why is that Baxter? Is it because she's worth more now?"

"She always had value to me." He wanted to reach out and pop her upside the head like Doc did him, but he was confident that would land him in jail. "You're only interested in a commission."

"It would seem that way, but that's not exactly the truth. I want her to be the best she can be. Few artists get a second chance at being great. Sosie was an amazing child artist, but then, as an adult, she was just another artist." She pointed at the canvases. "With these, she has a chance to be known as one of the greatest artists of her time, and Myron Straight can do that for her."

"Is that what she wants?"

Theresa laughed. "It's all she ever wanted. Myron will take her under his wing, and her paintings will be everywhere that counts. Why do you think she asked you to come?"

The weight of a sledgehammer hit his chest. "She wanted me to share in the joy of her success."

"She could have just told you it was fabulous, but you're

here so you can see how important this is to her. You know she packed up her place and put her things in storage."

"She what?" Bile rose and burned his throat.

"She'll tell you tonight. She's following her dream. Will you support her or stand in her way?"

Theresa walked away, and he leaned against a pillar for support.

He watched the animated conversation Sosie was having with Myron. She laughed and smiled and seemed to light up in his presence.

She turned toward him and winked, then raised a finger as if to say one more minute. He watched as she shook the man's hand. The kind of shake that happens when an agreement is reached.

Was Theresa right? Was Sosie on her journey back to greatness? It was quite a story with her going from being a famous child artist to blending in with the masses, then becoming blind and painting her best stuff. Would his presence be a detriment to her success?

"Sorry," she threaded her fingers with his. "Have you looked at the art?"

"Most." She led him through the gallery and pointed out the artists and why they were important to the art world.

"Can I ask you something?"

She leaned into his side. "We have no secrets. Ask anything."

"Did you give up your apartment and pack up your stuff?"

Her face fell. "Theresa," she said with disgust and a shake of her head. "She told you? It wasn't her place."

A woman walked over. "Sosie, we need you for a moment."

She looked at him and sighed. "Wait here, I'll be right back." She walked away and disappeared into the crowd.

He moved along the wall where her art hung and noticed they had sold all the pieces. Everything she set out to do, she'd accomplished. She delivered the art she was contracted to create, and there was no doubt she'd made enough to pay back the commission to the Albrights, but maybe she'd complete the project now that she could.

Theresa's words kept running through his head. *Where will you take her?*

"Down, I'll bring her down."

"Excuse me?" An older woman asked.

"Oh, nothing. Just thinking out loud."

"If you're thinking this woman has the world at the tip of her paintbrush, you're right. The art world is her oyster."

Baxter heard Sosie's sweet laughter and knew this was where she belonged. His original plan to tell her he'd move here would only stifle her progress as an artist. She'd need to move around to be successful, but he knew she'd feel obligated to stay with him.

Theresa was right; he'd only weigh her down. If he loved her, he'd turn around and leave. He took one last look at her blue eyes, her brilliant smile, and her art before he walked out.

CHAPTER TWENTY-ONE

Sosie finished her conversation and turned, expecting to find Baxter waiting for her, but he was gone. She made the rounds through the gallery twice, looking for him.

Smiling, as if she'd painted the art herself, was Theresa; speaking with a client about the *Love is Blind* piece.

"I'm sure I can get her to part with it. We all have a price."

Sosie marched over with her hands on her hips. "No, we don't all have a price." She turned to look at the man standing with Theresa. "I'm sorry, but this piece is not for sale." She laid her hand on her agent's arm and plastered on a smile. "Can I borrow you for a second?"

She didn't wait for Theresa to agree as she pulled her away from the crowd.

"Let's get this straight. That picture is not for sale. It belongs to Baxter."

Theresa rolled her eyes. "Oh, please, that man wouldn't know a masterpiece if it was staring him in the face. He probably thinks Legos are sculptures, and Spirograph is art."

Sosie laughed. "They could be." Baxter might not know a lot about art, but he knew her, and he appreciated what she did. He even supported her in a way that no one had, including her agent, who demanded the canvases but offered no suggestions on how to complete the project. "Do you know where he is. Last time I saw him, he was chatting with you."

Theresa inhaled. "How was your talk with Myron?"

Deflection was Theresa's superpower. She obviously didn't want to talk about Baxter and was pushing the conversation in a different direction. Sosie assumed Baxter had gone to the restroom, and she would see him in a moment. That's why she allowed Theresa to move the conversation to Myron.

"He's a nice man, but I'm not signing on with him. What's the deal with you two? I've never known you to turn over clients. What's your percentage on his take?"

"As long as it doesn't affect your paycheck, what do you care?"

She knew there had to be something in it for Theresa. She'd slowed down lately as one does when they age, and she wondered if this was the new arrangement Theresa was making with all her clients. She'd act as the middleman, but Myron and the artist would do all the work.

"I care because you're selling me like a pig to slaughter, and I'm not interested. I told you I'm not signing on for another year, or another minute, or another breath. You and I are finished after this show."

Theresa waved her finger in the air. "Not so fast, you have the Albright's to think about."

"Not true, I've contacted them and explained my situation. They've agreed to a refund of the earnest money and are contacting Juliette McKinnon to take on the project."

Could someone's cheeks turn so red and not cause a heart attack? "Juliette? I don't represent Juliette. You don't get to renegotiate contracts. That's my job."

"You're right. You're fired." She looked around for Baxter,

wondering where he could have gotten off to. "I'll make sure the gallery pays your percentage."

"You can't do this!" Her voice was so loud, most people within twenty feet of them turned to watch the drama unfolding. "You are worth more than that man can give you."

A chill raced through her and settled in her chest. "What did you do?"

"I did what had to be done. I told him the truth."

The heat was back, burning from her gut to her face. "What did you say to him?" She frantically searched the crowd, looking for the only friendly face she knew.

"I told him he had nothing to offer you. You know that's the truth. The man is an albatross around your neck, and he'll only hold you back."

"Oh my God, how could you?" Her pitch was high enough to shatter glass. "That man is why I have anything to sell at this show. Unlike you, he didn't abandon me. He was there for me the whole time."

Theresa looked around her. "He's not here now."

"Because you lied to him. What did you tell him?"

"I told him Myron was your future, and he was your past. I may have mentioned that you packed up your home. I can't help it if he thought something different."

Sosie's flat hand cracked against Theresa's cheek. She'd never slapped anyone in her life, but Theresa had it coming to her for years.

"You made it sound like I was leaving with Myron?"

Theresa rubbed the sting from her cheek. "It's for the better, Sosie. This show put you back on the map."

Sosie knew she needed to leave before she full-on tackled the bitch to the floor. She spun around and marched toward the gallery owner, who stood in the corner, eyes focused on the fight.

"My apologies." She smiled, even though her insides trembled. She knew she had an obligation to stay until the show was finished, but Mark Gallopoli had always been kind to her.

"I'd say this would be a great time to make a grand exit. People will talk about it for months or until the next time Theresa meddles in her artists' lives."

"I'm not her artist."

"No, you're not. I've got your new address in Aspen Cove, if anything changes, let me know, and I can forward your check to wherever you'd like." He moved down the aisle to *Love is Blind* and lifted it from the wall. "I think you have a delivery to make."

Sosie lifted on her tiptoes and kissed his cheek. "Thank you for understanding."

He laughed. "Who am I to stand in the way of love?" He passed the canvas to her. "Should you ever want to show your future work, just let me know, I'll always have a wall for you, Sosie."

Tears of gratefulness blurred her vision. It was bad enough that there were still cloudy halos, but now the downpour from her eyes made her almost as blind as she had been. She swiped at them and walked out the door.

Mark followed her and hailed the gallery's driver. "Take her to her hotel."

She eased the picture into the back seat of the Town Car and slid in behind it.

"Where to?" the driver asked.

"Brown Palace, please."

As soon as he pulled from the curb, she took her phone from her pocket and dialed Baxter. When it went to voice mail, she nearly wept. "Baxter, call me. It's not what you think."

What she needed to say to him couldn't be said over a message.

She called him once more before they reached the hotel, but remembered he was probably in a dead zone in the mountains on his way back home, and her calls wouldn't go through until he made it through the pass.

She thanked the driver as they neared the hotel. The valet opened her door, and she picked up the frame and rushed into the hotel.

At the front desk, she asked if they had a car service.

"We do, our driver can take you anywhere within a twenty-mile radius. Shall I call the car for you?"

"I need to go to Aspen Cove."

The woman's eyes grew wide. "That's over three hours away."

"I realize that, but it's a matter of"—she wanted to say life and death, but that seemed too dramatic—"importance."

"Important or not..." She looked at the clock behind her. "It's almost ten o'clock." It was an old-world clock. Something Sosie would have guessed hung exactly where it was when the hotel opened in 1895.

"People drive at ten o'clock."

"I'm sorry, we can't accommodate that distance." She opened a nearby drawer and pulled out several business cards. "You can try these companies." The woman put on her glad to be there face even though she probably wasn't. No one wanted to deal with a woman who held a canvas tied together by a checkered Vans shoelace and had tears spilling from her eyes. "Would you like me to call?"

Sosie nodded her head. "Can you? I really need to get there." Hoping she could pull at the girl's heartstrings, she said. "I need to deliver this painting to the man I love."

The girl lifted to look over the counter. "Don't you think candy and a sexy teddy would work better?"

Sosie laughed. "Probably, but I was just offered over a hundred grand for this painting, and I turned it down because his love is worth more."

"Go pack, and I'll see what I can do, Ms. Grant."

Sosie leaned in to focus on the woman's nametag. "Tessa, I can't thank you enough."

She dashed across the marble floors to the elevator and pressed the button. Why was it when she was in a hurry, everything moved like cold molasses?

The brass arrow of the turn of the century elevator swept a half-circle until it stopped on the ground floor and opened.

She waited for the woman and her silly shaved standard poodle to exit, then stepped in, pressed floor 5 a half dozen times until the doors closed, and she rose. At her floor, she ran from the elevator like the bees they raised on the rooftop chased her.

Once the door was open, she moved around the room like an evacuee given a few minutes notice to leave.

Bag packed and sitting by the door, she plopped in a chair by the phone and waited, hoping Tessa came through. Waiting for the call was like watching an inchworm climb a mountain.

She figured if she left now, she could reasonably arrive in Aspen Cove in the early morning hours and climb into bed with Baxter.

After they made love, or before, depending on what he wanted and needed, she'd explain everything. She tapped her fingers on the nightstand and waited and waited.

Forty minutes later, the phone rang.

"It's not a limousine, but I've got you a ride."

"I'll be right down."

She swung her bag over her shoulder and grabbed the handle of her suitcase in one hand and the painting in the other.

Thankfully, the elevator was already waiting for her. Her heels *click-clacked* against the stone flooring as she hurried toward the front desk.

"Ms. Grant, over here." Tessa waved to her from the

revolving door. "So, I couldn't get a car for you at the last minute, but I found you transportation. Keep an open mind."

"What do you mean?"

"You'll see." She took Sosie's suitcase and walked out the door.

The only vehicle sitting in front of the valet was an old Volkswagen van covered in Dutch Brother stickers and peace signs.

"This is my ride?" She rubbed at her eyes, thinking she was seeing things.

"It's all I could come up with at the last minute."

A young guy with blond dreadlocks and a Rastafarian hat hopped out of the driver's side. He moved toward her, but instead of introducing himself to Sosie, he picked up Tessa and twirled her around. "Hey babe," He pressed his lips to Tessa's, and Sosie was certain the girl's knees buckled. "Is this my passenger?"

Tessa pulled away from him and turned around with a smile as bright as the sun. "Ms. Grant, this is my boyfriend River, and he'd be happy to take you to Aspen Cove if you pay for the gas."

Sosie looked at the van, which seemed held together by the stickers and a few strategically placed wires.

"I'm in." She would have strapped herself to the back of a moped if it was going her way.

River took her bag and tossed it in the back. When he grabbed for the painting, Tessa yelled, "No, apparently, that picture is worth a fortune."

River looked it over. "Some people will pay anything for crap."

Sosie laughed. She tucked the picture in the back of the van on top of the mattress that she didn't want to think about and moved back to Tessa.

"Thank you."

The girl blushed. "No problem, I'm a sucker for love." After a quick hug of appreciation, Sosie climbed in the passenger seat, littered with empty organic yogurt containers. She kicked them aside, making room for her feet, and shut the door.

While Tessa gave River an over the top goodbye kiss, Sosie pulled out her phone and tried Baxter again. If she was lucky, she'd get him in one of the few places where a bar or two popped in.

It went directly to voice mail. She sighed and hung up. Instead, she texted him.

You promised to never leave me. I need to talk to you. I'm on my way. I love you.

River climbed into the driver's seat and turned the key. The van spit and sputtered, then died.

"Don't worry, she's a finicky girl, but she's never let me down." He reached his hand out and rubbed the dash like it was a lover. He pumped the gas twice and twisted the key again; it growled and groaned and caught. The van coughed and passed clouds of dark smoke for the first block, but they were on their way.

"Care to listen to music?"

She nodded. Music would at least occupy her mind. "Sounds great."

He turned the knob of the old radio and tuned into a station playing Bob Marley. Of course, it would be *One Love* because she was on her way to hers.

They made decent time until they hit the mountain roads. The van bogged down as they climbed in elevation.

River spoke words of affirmation to his van, which he called Buttercup. "Come on, baby, come on. You can do it. At the top, you get to coast until the next climb."

Sosie was questioning her decision to climb into a van that was probably rescued from the junkyard.

Buttercup made it to the crest and coasted over several hills for the next two hours, but the final pass proved to be a challenge. They were chugging along when a loud pop sounded, and River struggled to keep the beast on the road.

"Well, I think that might end our adventure." He pulled the limping vehicle to the side of the road and exited. "Yep," he yelled. "Tire's blown."

"No, no, no," she chanted, climbing out to look. "Don't you have a spare?"

He laughed. "I can't afford a spare." He looked up at the big pines looming over them like giants. "This seems as good a place to bed down for the night. I'm sure we can flag someone over in the morning."

"Bed down. No way. I have to get to Aspen Cove." She marched to the passenger side and got her purse. A look at her phone told her they were in a dead zone.

She opened the back of the van and took out her suitcase. Tossing it to the ground, she opened it and began removing her clothes. "Do you think Tessa would want these?" She held up several shirts and pants, things that had cost a fortune in their day, but didn't have any value to her now.

"Not sure, but you can leave them behind." He picked up a sexy nightgown and smiled. "Now we're talking."

"That one is coming with me." She snatched it from him and tucked it back into her bag. Once she had room for the canvas, she tucked it into the empty side and closed it back up.

"You're not going to walk, are you?" He pointed to her heels.

She growled and opened her suitcase again to change into her checkered Vans. "I'm getting to Baxter one way or another. Even if I have to ride a grizzly into town, I'm going."

"Right on." He rummaged through the trash cluttered space between the seats and pulled out a bottle of water and a bag of nuts. "You'll need to keep up your energy. You've got about twenty miles to go." He held up the baggie of nuts. "These are from the pines around here. I picked them and toasted them myself."

"Are they safe?"

"The animals eat them."

Animals ate their own poop at times too, but she didn't have time to argue. She pulled out the twenties she had in her wallet. Funnily enough, she'd folded them in half twice like she learned from LightHouse. "This is all I have on me. I'm sorry to leave you stranded."

"It's all good." He pointed to the van. "I've got a sweet mattress and some weed. I'll be fine. If you make it to Aspen Cove, can you call Tessa and tell her where I am?"

If I make it?

"I will make it, and as soon as I get a signal, I'll call her."

Sosie set off on the longest walk of her life. How far would she travel for love? To the ends of the earth.

CHAPTER TWENTY-TWO

Baxter woke with his head pounding and his heart aching. Once he left the gallery, he headed straight home. At one point, he considered turning around and going back, but begging wouldn't be good for either of them. It would guilt her into staying, and it would make him feel like she stuck around to make him feel better. Sosie was that kind of woman; she was kindhearted and loving and giving. Hell, she'd bought her mom a home and sent her brother to rehab when she was at her lowest. She put others first, and he didn't want her to sacrifice her future for him.

He almost called her last night because going to bed wasn't the same without hearing her tell him she loved him, and he was certain she did, but when he looked at his phone, the battery was dead.

He rolled onto his back and took several breaths.

"I lived without her before, and I'll live without her again." The words sounded hollow because living without Sosie wasn't living at all.

He glanced at his phone to find several messages. His heart soared when he listened to the voice mail.

Baxter, call me. It's not what you think.

What the hell? He jumped up from the bed and dialed her number.

"You've reached Sosie, you know what to do."

He tugged on his jeans and scrolled through her texts.

You promised to never leave me. I need to talk to you. I'm on my way. I love you.

The time the text came in was over five hours ago. If she were on her way, she'd be there. He pulled on a shirt, slipped on his shoes, grabbed his keys, and ran down the stairs. He nearly ran Katie over on his way out.

"Have you seen Sosie?"

She shifted the supplies in her hands and opened the door to the bakery. "No, she hasn't been back that I know of."

"Thanks," he ran around the building and into the diner. He scanned the room, looking for the prettiest girl in the world, but she wasn't there.

"Can I get you something, Baxter?" Aunt Maisey asked.

"Looking for Sosie. Have you seen her?" His aunt looked at him with concern. "I thought she went back to Denver."

"She did," he turned to leave but called a thanks over his shoulder.

He jogged back to his truck and took off toward the studio. When he got there, the lights were off, and no one was in the building.

Sitting in his truck, he ran through all the options he had. He didn't know anyone in Denver who could check in with her. The only name that came to mind was Theresa, but she didn't like him much, and he was certain she wouldn't give him any information.

Without options, he looked her agency up and dialed.

"Branton Agency, this is Melissa, can I help you?"

"Can I speak to Theresa, please?"

"Who's calling?"

"Baxter Black."

There was a moment of silence while she put him on hold, and then the phone clicked over.

"Calling to gloat?"

"What? I don't know what you're talking about."

He heard the woman let out a growl. "Sure, you do, she chose you over everything. I handed her a perfect life on a silver platter, and she wanted you instead."

His insides twisted. Something was very wrong. "What the hell are you going on about?"

"Sosie left the gallery to go after you. She chose love over a life that would bring her everything."

His heart filled to bursting. She'd chosen him. "Where is she?"

Several long seconds passed. "Isn't she with you? I would have sworn she would have checked out of the Brown Palace and headed straight for Aspen Cove."

He hung up without saying another word. His next call was to the Brown Palace Hotel. "Sosie Grant's room, please."

"I'm sorry sir, Ms. Grant checked out last night."

"Are you sure?"

The woman's voice got muffled. "Yes, I'm sure. Tessa was in a titter about how her boyfriend was driving Sosie to Aspen Cove to chase love. The girl is such a romantic."

"Thank you." He put his truck in gear and headed back toward Denver. All clues pointed to her returning, but she never made it, so something had to have happened.

He wound through town and hopped on the highway that led to Denver. About six miles in, he saw her walking on the soft shoulder, looking like she'd run a marathon. Behind her, she tugged her suitcase. She didn't notice him slow down and pull a U-turn to come up behind her.

He rolled down the window. "Hey, lady, do you need a ride?"

She stopped and looked up. Beads of sweat poured down her face, and smudges of road dust streaked her cheeks.

"Baxter?" Her voice was gravelly. "Is that you?" She rubbed her eyes as if she were seeing a mirage.

He was out of the truck in seconds, sweeping her into his arms. "You crazy woman. What are you doing?"

"I'm trying to get back to you. Do you have any idea how hard it's been?" She lifted her tennis shoe. "These are not made for rough terrain." She pointed to the torn seam on her blue dress. "Not really hiking clothes either." She pressed her lower lip out in a pout. "And about five miles back, I dropped my pine nuts, and a damn squirrel came out of nowhere and swiped the whole bag." Her voice quivered, and her shoulders shook. "Take me home."

"You got it." He put her bag in the back of the truck and helped her inside.

As he drove, he held onto her hand, afraid if he let go, she'd disappear.

"What happened Sosie? I thought you would head to Paris with that Myron guy."

"When we get home, the first thing I'm doing is kissing you, but after that, I'm beating some sense into you. Why would I choose him when I have you?"

Baxter gripped the wheel so tightly his knuckles tingled. "He can give you everything you ever wanted."

She shook her head. "No, he can't give me your love. That's all I want. All I need."

"But Theresa said—"

"Theresa is an idiot. Why you listened to her, I don't understand. You could have asked me."

He felt like an idiot. He should have asked her.

"I didn't want you to sacrifice your career for a life with me."

"Isn't it time I sacrificed my career for a life? I've been

waiting for you to show up for years. Why did you take so long?"

He pulled into town and parked behind the apartment. When he killed the engine, he turned to her. "I've been looking for the right woman in the wrong place. Who knew she'd show up on my doorstep?"

"Will you share your life with me, Baxter?"

He chuckled. "Is that a proposal?"

"Would you say yes if it was?"

He rubbed his chin. "Do you have a ring?"

She looked behind her at the suitcase in the truck's bed. "No, but I have a painting worth a hundred grand."

His jaw nearly hit his chest. "You brought the painting?"

She unbuckled and scooted next to him. "It was yours."

"But it said it was reserved. I thought you'd sold it."

She straddled his lap. Pressed between the steering wheel and him, there wasn't much room for maneuvering.

"It was always yours. I gave it to you."

He cupped her cheek. "Not really, I kind of claimed it."

"True, but it was yours from the day you saw it."

He pressed his lips to hers. "You were mine from the day I saw you."

"Liar, you didn't even like me."

"I didn't know you, but that first night I climbed into your bed to comfort you ... I knew I'd never want to leave."

"That's the night I fell in love. You showed me more compassion and caring than I've ever known."

"You look exhausted."

"I'm totally spent and ready for bed, but not for sleep."

He looked into her eyes and saw passion and fire there. "Let's get you cleaned up, fed, and fully satisfied."

She frowned. "Do you have to work today?"

He shook his head. "No, I don't have to work, but, I will

work all day pleasing you, and then wake up tomorrow and do it again."

He opened the door and climbed out of the cab with her attached to him. She raised her legs to wrap them around his waist and held on tightly to his neck. He made it halfway to the door before he turned around.

"I should get my ring before someone steals it."

She laughed so hard, she couldn't hold on to him and slid down his body. "So, is that a yes?"

"Are you really asking?" He grabbed her suitcase and carried it upstairs.

"Are you saying yes?"

He patted her bottom. "Get upstairs, future Mrs. Black."

She squealed and ran up the stairs in front of him.

How did his life move from colorless to filled with every hue under the rainbow? It was because a blind artist filled her paintbrush with love and brought brightness into his life.

CHAPTER TWENTY-THREE

ONE WEEK LATER.

"What do you think?" She danced around the living room of her new home.

"Are you sure we should put that picture on the mantel?" Baxter asked. "I mean, it's worth a fortune."

She shook her head. "It's only worth what someone will pay for it."

"I know, and you said someone offered you a hundred grand."

"Do you want to sell it?" She knew if he did, Baxter could afford all the bells and whistles he ever dreamed for their home. *Their home.*

"No way, this picture has more emotional value than it could ever have monetary value. You painted it on the first day of the rest of your life."

"No, that day was when I made you wear your mashed potatoes and gravy."

"True, but the answer is still no. I love what it represents. It was a new beginning. You took a risk on me, and yourself, and now we have a painting worth more than the house it's hanging in."

She moved to him and wrapped her arms around his waist. "Not true, there's no value great enough to put on a house filled with love."

She moved through the living room, full of furniture from her apartment. It was fine for now, but as they grew together, they would make everything theirs.

"Are you ready to head to lunch with the band?" Samantha had invited everyone who rented space at The Guild Creative Center to lunch catered by Dalton.

He frowned. "I'm not sure I want to share you with anyone. Did you know that Red had the hots for you that day you helped with his house?"

"Really?" She took her bag from the coffee table and slung it over her shoulder.

"Yes." He followed her to the door.

"He's not really my type. I like them tall, dark, and dashing. They have to be able to tell aqua from turquoise and tomato red from scarlet. They have to kiss like Romeo and make love like a god. It also doesn't hurt if they can cook a meal or do a load of laundry. The icing on the cake is when they value their woman more for the love she brings than the art she sells. Add to that, the skill of making her see everything so clearly when she couldn't see at all—that's pure relationship magic."

"Just call me Houdini." They climbed into the truck and drove toward The Guild Creative Center. On their way, they passed Axel's house.

"Is that Mercy?" Sosie watched the woman tuck a pair of pink lace panties in the chain-link fence.

Baxter slowed, and Mercy's eyes opened wide. She tugged the panties free and moved down the sidewalk, pulling the other ten pair from between the links.

Baxter rolled down his window. "Everything okay?"

"Disgusting. Can you believe women leave their underwear on the fence?" She huffed. "There are children in this neighborhood." She opened the neighbor's trash can and tossed them all inside. "Somebody has to be the voice of reason."

"Carry on," Baxter said. He drove forward, but Sosie turned around to see Mercy pull the pink panties from the trash can and tuck them into the fence before she ran off.

Next up is One Hundred Lessons

OTHER BOOKS BY KELLY COLLINS

Recipes for Love

A Tablespoon of Temptation

A Pinch of Passion

A Dash of Desire

A Cup of Compassion

A Dollop of Delight

A Layer of Love

Recipe for Love Collection 1-3

The Second Chance Series

Set Free

Set Aside

Set in Stone

Set Up

Set on You

The Second Chance Series Box Set

A Pure Decadence Series

Yours to Have

Yours to Conquer

Yours to Protect

A Pure Decadence Collection

Wilde Love Series

Betting On Him

Betting On Her

Betting On Us

A Wilde Love Collection

The Boys of Fury Series

Redeeming Ryker

Saving Silas

Delivering Decker

The Boys of Fury Boxset

Making the Grade Series

The Dean's List

Honor Roll

The Learning Curve

Making the Grade Box Set

Stand Alone Billionaire Novels

Dream Maker

JOIN MY READER'S CLUB AND GET A FREE BOOK.

Go to www.authorkellycollins.com

ABOUT THE AUTHOR

International bestselling author of more than thirty novels, Kelly Collins writes with the intention of keeping love alive. Always a romantic, she blends real-life events with her vivid imagination to create characters and stories that lovers of contemporary romance, new adult, and romantic suspense will return to again and again.

For More Information
www.authorkellycollins.com
kelly@authorkellycollins.com

Printed in Great Britain
by Amazon

38077017R00109